Pibroch

and Other Sheiling Stories

NEIL MUNRO

With an introduction by Ronnie Renton
Notes by Rennie McOwan and Rae MacGregor

British Library Cataloguing in Publication Data
A catalogue record of this book is available from the British Library

ISBN 1 899863 10 9

First published 1896

© Text, Neil Munro, 1996
© Introduction and Notes, Ronnie Renton, Rennie McOwan and Rae MacGregor, 1996

Typeset by XL Publishing Services, Nairn
Printed in Great Britain
by BPC-AUP Aberdeen Ltd
for House of Lochar
Isle of Colonsay, Argyll PA61 7YR

Contents

Introduction

NEIL MUNRO (1863–1930)

Neil Munro was born in the little town of Inveraray near the head of Loch Fyne in Argyll, an area of exceptional beauty which was to influence him all his life. He was born to Ann Munro, a kitchen maid, perhaps at Inveraray Castle, in the building known as Crombie's Land on 3rd June 1863. Soon after, Neil and his mother moved in with his grandmother Anne McArthur Munro who lived in a one-roomed house in McVicar's Land (now known as Arkland II). His grandmother hailed from Bailemeanoch on Loch Aweside and she brought up Neil's mother in Glen Aray in the landward part of Inveraray parish on a farm called Ladyfield. Both were native speakers of Gaelic and it is from them that the young Neil received his knowledge of the old language and culture. Indeed, he spent much of his childhood in Glen Aray and it was to become the setting for many of the tales in his *The Lost Pibroch and Other Sheiling Stories*. It seems likely also that Neil lived for some of his life in accommodation in Inveraray jail. His mother appears to have been employed there and in 1875 she married Malcolm Thomson, the governor, after he had retired.

Although he was to go on to be one of the outstanding literary figures of his day Neil Munro did not attend university. He was educated at the parish school in Inveraray under the tutelage of the scholarly Henry Dunn Smith with some periods spent at the little school in Glen Aray where the teacher John McArthur taught the Bible in Gaelic. When he left school in 1877 he gained appointment as a clerk in the office of William Douglas, a local lawyer who was to become the model for Dan Dyce in the novel *The Daft Days* (1907). Whilst working there he learned what Latin he knew from Traynor's *Maxims* and also taught himself shorthand. Even at this stage he seems to have been preparing himself for a career in journalism. As for so many young Gaels in these days, however, good careers were hard to come by in the Highlands and on the 1st June 1881, two days before his eighteenth birthday, he emigrated to Glasgow in search of better prospects but never forgot Inveraray or Argyll – they were to feed his imagination for the rest of his life.

After a brief spell as cashier in a firm of ironmongers he soon moved into journalism to become successively reporter on *The Greenock Advertiser*, *The Glasgow News*, the *Falkirk Herald* and, finally, the *Glasgow Evening News* where he was made chief reporter under editor James

Murray Smith at the age of only 23. In the meantime he had married Jessie Adam, the daughter of his landlady in North Woodside Road.

In addition to his journalistic writing he tried his hand at a thriller and also sent humorous sketches to the London paper *The Globe* but he was to make his first real mark on the literary scene in 1896 with the publication of his completely innovative collection *The Lost Pibroch and Other Sheiling Stories*. These were soon followed after its serialisation in *Blackwood's Magazine* by the publication in book form of his first novel *John Splendid* (1898) – which could be argued to be the first truly authentic Highland novel. Like most of Munro's novels it is set in a period of major social change. It deals with the sack of Inveraray by Montrose and his subsequent victory at the battle of Inverlochy in 1645. It also explores the Highland character under stress, particularly in the persons of Gillesbeg Gruamach, the Marquis of Argyll, who is anxious to move on from clan warfare to the more peaceful ways of commerce and the rule of law, and his clansman Iain Alainn, John Splendid himself, a swaggering *miles gloriosus* figure whose loyalty permits him to humour his chief and yield to his whims until, finally convinced of his cowardice, he rebels.

After *John Splendid* had been accepted for serialisation in 1897 Munro reduced his journalism to the part-time commitment of two weekly columns to the *Glasgow Evening News* called "The Looker On" and "Views and Reviews". This was to allow him to concentrate on his literary work and in 1899 the novel *Gilian the Dreamer* was published. Again set in Inveraray at a time of social change – the aftermath of the Napoleonic wars – the story tells of a young boy Gilian who has creative gifts which in an earlier Highland society might have been nurtured to enable him to become a bard but the old Gaelic tradition has been broken and Gilian's gifts merely manifest themselves in excessive sensibility and self-indulgent dreaming which impede his maturity and his ability to act effectively. He has affinities with Tommy Sandys in J. M. Barrie's *Sentimental Tommy* (1896) and his failure to grow up properly also makes him a kind of Highland Peter Pan.

His next three novels were all to be loosely connected with the aftermath of the Jacobite Rising of 1745. *Doom Castle* (1901) takes its inspiration from Dundarave Castle on the shores of Loch Fyne. On one level it is a Gothic tale of intrigue and romance but at a deeper level it shows the hopelessness of the Jacobite cause in the face of the new Hanoverian order – a hopelessness symbolised by the decaying castle of the Baron of Doom compared with the fine Enlightenment castle of the Duke of Argyll in Inveraray. *The Shoes of Fortune* (1901), unusually for Munro, has its setting in Lowland Scotland and in France. It deals with the death throes of the Jacobite movement as it makes a final bid to join the French in an invasion of Britain. The hero Paul Greig, having seen the antics of the dissolute and broken Prince Charles Edward, renounces his Jacobitism and warns Pitt, thus preventing the invasion. The final novel of this period, *Children of Tempest* (1903) is only loosely connected with the '45 Rising. It is set on South Uist and deals with the Loch Arkaig treasure, French money which had been intended to support the Rising but had mysteriously been moved to a cave on the island of Mingulay. This becomes an object of greed and leads to the kidnapping of the heroine and the death of the villain and his *incubus* in a dramatic scene on the cliffs of Mingulay.

At this point in his writing career Neil Munro clearly felt that he had carried the theme of historical romance far enough and the next novels mark a major change of direction. Before we deal with them, however, it should be observed that one character from *Children of Tempest* obviously provided a special source of enjoyment for him. He was Captain Dan MacNeil, the skipper of the "Happy Return", and he could well be the prototype of that other master mariner who was to make Munro a household name for generations to come – Para Handy. The first of the hilarious Para Handy stories was published in 1905 in the "Looker On" column of the *Glasgow Evening News* and Munro continued writing these for most of his working life. He published them in three book collections: *The Vital Spark* (1906), *In Highland Harbours* (1911) and *Hurricane Jack of the Vital Spark* (1923). "The Looker On" had earlier also been the original place of publication for the humorous sketches about Erchie MacPherson, the beadle and waiter who had comments on everything from prohibition to The Glasgow Girls (artists), and which were published in book form under the title *Erchie, My Droll Friend* in 1904. This column was also to host the sketches of the big hearted commercial traveller Jimmy Swan, the first of which appeared in 1911. These were produced in book form in 1917 under the title *Jimmy Swan, The Joy Traveller*. All of these humorous tales appeared under the name of Hugh Foulis, the author keeping his own name for what he considered to be his more important literary creations. He did not, however, use all of these stories for the book editions published in his lifetime and it is only with very recent editions of *Para Handy*, (Birlinn, Edinburgh, 1992) and *Erchie & Jimmy Swann* (Birlinn, Edinburgh, 1993), excellently researched by Brian Osborne and Ronald Armstrong, that we have come to appreciate fully just how many of these he wrote for "The Looker On" column. This is especially true of the Erchie stories, most of which were not written until after Munro's own 1904 edition.

In 1907 *The Clyde, River and Firth*, a beautiful travelogue with painted illustrations by Mary Y. and J. Young Hunter, appeared as did his next novel *The Daft Days*. As noted above Munro had decided to move away from historical romance and so this latest novel deals with the contemporary scene. It has all the superficial appearance of a Kailyard novel and yet is a subtle subversion of that genre. It is the story of a little American girl, Bud, who has lost her parents and comes to stay with her relatives in a small Scottish town (clearly based on Inveraray). She progresses, thanks to her enlightened but only semi-liberated Aunt Ailie, to become a Shakespearean actress in London's West End – in spite of the negativity of the Scottish education system and the background of social and religious attitudes which regarded the theatre as unsuitable and rather sinful. It is especially interesting because it confronts the problem of the female creative artist in a society whose mores inhibit the expression of her talent.

By now his literary reputation was quite secure and in 1908 he was honoured with an LLD from the University of Glasgow. This was followed the next year with the award of the Freedom of Inveraray.

In 1910 he published *Fancy Farm*, at once his least successful novel and yet in some ways his most ambitious and one on which he is known to have exercised much time and care. It is very much a novel of ideas and is a satire on the political philosophy of its hero, the Laird of Schawfield, who appears to be at one with nature and attempts to run his estate on egalitarian lines – only to find that a young lady of whom he thinks he is enamoured can run it better. The plot, however, is confusing at times. Much more successful was the short story collection *Ayrshire Idylls* which appeared in 1912. These sketches were published by A. & C. Black and illustrated by the drawings and watercolour landscape paintings of George Houston. They show Munro very much at home in a Lowland Ayrshire setting and among other interesting items contain four stories which reconstruct incidents from the life of Burns and two effectively depicted Covenanting tales.

Neil Munro's most accomplished novel, however, and also his last was *The New Road* (1914) and, not surprisingly after the disappointment of *Fancy Farm*, we find him returning to the historical genre. This is the story of the young Aeneas MacMaster's quest for knowledge about the mysterious death of his Jacobite father, Paul. We are kept in suspense until the last page before the mystery is fully unfolded and we learn all the treachery and double-dealing of Sandy Duncanson, the factor who had murdered Paul and made himself owner of Aeneas's rightful inheritance. But it is much more than an eighteenth century whodunnit. Like Walter Scott's *Waverley* this novel deals with the gradual disillusionment of the hero Aeneas with the romantic glamour of the Highlands. He is made to see through the romantic reputation of Highland chiefs like Barisdale and Lovat and gets to know them for the scoundrels that they are. Like his merchant uncle he comes to believe that only by trade and commerce will the Highlands ultimately be civilised and the means of achieving this will be the New Road which Wade is building between Stirling and Inverness. This road becomes a symbol of a more civilised and prosperous way of life for the Highlands, but, at the same time, things will be utterly changed by it and it will mean the loss of the whole ancient Gaelic way of life. This is a powerful novel about the forces which shape the destinies of individuals. It is great historical fiction!

With the outbreak of the First World War Neil Munro returned to full time journalism. He also visited the Front on four occasions as a war correspondent but the most traumatic event of the war for him was the loss of his son Hugh at Loos in 1915. This loss coupled with the pressure of work on the paper – he became editor of the *Glasgow Evening News* in 1918 on the retiral of James Murray Smith – seemed to inhibit any more large scale literary production. He did, however, publish the urbane and witty short story collection *Jaunty Jock and Other Stories* in 1917, although many of these would have been written before the war. The typescript of the first ten chapters of a novel with the working title *The Search* also survives. It is a sequel to *The New Road* and is set just after Culloden. It is a stirring opening and it would be interesting to know why the story was never completed.

Journalist, critic and novelist, he was also a poet. In 1931, after his death, John Buchan edited a collection of his poetry for Blackwood. These poems had appeared throughout his life in magazines, newspapers and as parts of his novels. There are some fine pieces among them, especially "The Only Son" which is a thinly disguised lament for his son Hugh. They do not, however, have the quality of his prose. Indeed, Buchan comments: "His prose seems to me more strictly poetic than his verse."

In 1927 Neil Munro's health was failing. He retired from the *Glasgow Evening News* reluctantly for he enjoyed his work and the camaraderie of his colleagues. Indeed, he was without doubt the most affable and kindest of men. But even in retirement he continued to work. His last book was a *History of the Royal Bank of Scotland* (1928) and he continued to write articles, "Random Reminiscences", under the soubriquet Mr Incognito for the *Daily Record and Mail*. In October, 1930 he was honoured with a second LLD, this time by the University of Edinburgh, but sadly at the ceremony he was in obvious ill health. He died a few months later on 22nd December at his home "Cromalt" in Craigendoran, Helensburgh. He was survived by his wife Jessie, one son and four daughters.

In 1935 An Comunn Gaidhealach erected a monument to him at the head of Glen Aray. The decoration at the top of the simple column is in the shape of a Celtic book shrine and on it is the Gaelic inscription "Sar Litreachas" – "Excellent Literature". Among those present at the ceremony were many friends and admirers including Sir Harry Lauder. In his address the writer R. B. Cunninghame Graham praised Neil Munro as "the apostolic successor of Sir Walter Scott". A fitting tribute!

THE LOST PIBROCH AND OTHER SHEILING STORIES (1896)

In a letter to his publisher Blackwood of 26th February, 1894 concerning the possibility of submitting a volume of Highland short stories for publication Neil Munro wrote as follows:

... I shall be only too glad to lay before you at some early date, for your consideration, such a number of West Highland stories as might make a volume. I am not the most impartial judge, perhaps, but I have a strong belief, amounting almost to a certainty, that my sketches have something of the stuff of popularity in them. They strike upon a field absolutely untouched for one thing, being purely Celtic in their treatment of the Highland Celt and Highland scenery whereas all the men who have dealt with the romance of the Highlands hitherto have been Lowlanders, writing from the outside. The Barrie – Crockett – MacLaren "boom" has confined itself to the Lowlands; the stuff they deal with is becoming attenuated and run to seed. Here – or I am a Dutchman! – is a new vein, rich and untried.

From this it is very clear that Munro was well aware of the current state of Scottish writing. To take the latter part first, it is obvious that he was well aware of the limitations of the sentimental Lowland "Kailyard" writing represented by the early work of Barrie and Crockett and, particularly, by the stories in *Beside the Bonnie Briar Bush* (1894) of "Ian MacLaren" (Rev. John Watson). He had no intention of imitating their sentimental approach. Secondly, he draws attention to the fact that all previous writers who have dealt with "the romance of the Highlands" have no real feel for the subject. They have been "Lowlanders, writing from the outside", the creators of the Celtic Twilight, especially the extravagantly mystical "Fiona MacLeod", the pen-name of William Sharp, the Paisley novelist. As a native Gael Munro feels he can redress that balance.

It is with all this in mind that Neil Munro, a Highlander familiar with the Gaelic tradition, explores this "new vein, rich and untried" of Scottish literature as he seeks to give a more genuine and unsentimental account of the Highlands and the Highlander in his first collection of short stories *The Lost Pibroch and Other Sheiling Stories* in 1896.

A major feature in his attempt to represent the Gael more accurately is his special use of language. In the past, even writers like Hogg and Scott had represented the Gael's tongue in such a way that was at best inaccurate and at worst parodic and condescending as the following illustrates:

"Na, na, Hughie Morrison is no the man fo pargains – ye maun come to some Highland body like Robin Oig hersell fo the like of these – put I maun pe wishing you goot night..." (From *The Two Drovers* by Sir Walter Scott)

Munro rejected this utterly. Instead he moved to much more authentic Gaelic-English, influenced by the translations of *Popular Tales of the West Highlands* (1860-62) by the polymath and scholar John Francis Campbell of Islay, Iain Og Ile. This involved the frequent retention of Gaelic syntax in the English translation except, of course, that Munro's stories were not translations but fresh creations. Obviously it would be impossible to write whole sentences or paragraphs this way but he does it sufficiently often to give the flavour of Gaelic language structures e.g.

"...it's lame he'll be all his days anyway, and little use to any man." ("Black Murdo")

In addition, he frequently incorporates specific Gaelic idioms e.g. "the mouth of the night" literally translates "beul na h-oidhche" and means "twilight", and throughout the text there is gentle spattering of actual Gaelic words though not so many as to hold up the reader's progress e.g. *caman* (shinty stick), *iolair* (eagle), etc. He also incorporates an abundance of Gaelic place names. Other not strictly linguistic features such as use of proverbs (many of them genuine) and the names of well known pipe tunes also enhance the Gaelic atmosphere. Furthermore – and a point not often noted – he includes a wide range of Scots words which would have infiltrated the Highland speech of Inveraray and its environs long before standard English.

The effect of all this is to create the illusion for the reader that s/he is initiated into the language and culture of the characters in much the same way that Lewis Grassic Gibbon's "Speak of the Mearns" takes us into the world of his East Coast region, the main difference being that Munro's task is more difficult since he has a completely separate language to represent as opposed to a dialect of Scots.

The collection *The Lost Pibroch and Other Sheiling Stories* consists of twelve tales. Superficially they have the appearance of the tales of oral tradition and it is natural that Munro chose the folk tale model since it was the dominant prose genre in the Gaelic literature of the time, the modern short story not yet having been developed. Closer examination, however, reveals a much tauter structure than prevails in oral pieces and almost all are shot through and held together by a marvellous bitter irony. The setting (again unlike the traditional tale) is highly localised and almost every one of these stories is set in the area adjacent to Inveraray, especially Glen Aray.

The title story "The Lost Pibroch" is mysterious. In highly poetic language it tells of a piping competition in Half Town between two travelling pipers and Paruig Dall (Blind Peter). Eventually Paruig plays the tune "The Lost Pibroch" and its haunting music has a tremendously unsettling effect, first on the other two pipers, then on the men of Half Town, then on Paruig himself. All grow restless and depart and the women and children are left behind to fend for themselves in a derelict economy.

It is a difficult story to interpret. It is possible to see it as an allegory of the history of the Highlands depicting the dereliction of the Highland way of life after Culloden, the Clearances and the years of emigration to the cities, to Canada and elsewhere. The author appears to be hinting that the break up of the old Highland way of life is inevitable – a theme which persists throughout his later historical romances.

With the exception of "Jus PrimæNoctis" ("The Right of First Night"), a humorous tale which was rejected by Blackwood for the first edition because it was too risqué, and "Boboon's Children" which demonstrates the power of nature over nurture, the remaining nine stories are dark and bitter pieces. "The Fell Sergeant", "The Sea-Fairy of the French Foreland", "Shudderman Soldier" and the fantasy "Castle Dark" deal in various ways with love thwarted or unrequited. "Red Hand", "The Secret of the Heather-Ale", "Black Murdo", "War" and "A Fine Pair of Shoes" show how far people will go to protect pride of family or clan. Indeed, two of these – "Black Murdo" and "War" – come near to true tragedy in the Aristotelian sense in that the *hubris* or pride of the main character brings about appalling disaster, in the latter case, the death of an innocent child.

The Lost Pibroch and Other Sheiling Stories was enthusiastically received when it was issued in 1896 and there is no doubt that these stories in which the emphasis is frequently on action show a high degree of craftsmanship. Nonetheless, they are Munro's early work and they do, understandably, show some teething troubles, given that he was embarked on a completely new venture. As was shown above he was reacting against the sentimentality of the Kailyard and he wanted to paint a more authentic picture of the Gael than the Lowland purveyors of Celtic Twilight had done. In his endeavour to do so he anticipates George Douglas Brown's criticism of his own novel *The House with the Green Shutters* (1901) that "There is too much black for the white in it". Certainly, the grimness and savageness of "Red Hand", "Black Murdo" and even "The Secret of the Heather-Ale" are too "black" to be "natural". Also, the stories are often set in a past that has no clear historical context and this sometimes has the effect of producing vague, elemental, semi-Ossianic characters whose world lacks historical credibility. Having said that, the freshness of Neil Munro's approach with his detailed knowledge and love of Argyll and Gaelic tradition and his interesting experimentation with Gaelic-English constitutes a breakthrough in the representation of the Gael in non-Gaelic Scottish literature. The *Lost Pibroch* collection prepares the way for Munro's own very fine and carefully researched historical novel *John Splendid* which was to be issued the following year, for his other excellent historical romances, especially *Doom Castle* and *The New Road*, and for the Highland fiction of the Scottish Renaissance writers Neil Gunn and Fionn MacColla.

The Lost Pibroch

To the make of a piper go seven years of his own learning and seven generations before. If it is in, it will out, as the Gaelic old-word says; if not, let him take to the net or sword. At the end of his seven years one born to it will stand at the start of knowledge, and leaning a fond ear to the drone, he may have parley with old folks of old affairs. Playing the tune of the "Fairy Harp," he can hear his forefolks, plaided in skins, towsy-headed and terrible, grunting at the oars and snoring in the caves; he has his whittle and club in the "Desperate Battle" (my own tune, my darling!), where the white-haired sea-rovers are on the shore, and a stain's on the edge of the tide; or, trying his art on Laments, he can stand by the cairn of kings, ken the colour of Fingal's hair, and see the moon-glint on the hook of the Druids!

To-day there are but three pipers in the wide world, from the Sound of Sleat to the Wall of France. Who they are, and what their tartan, it is not for one to tell who has no heed for a thousand dirks in his doublet, but they may be known by the lucky ones who hear them. Namely players tickle the chanter and take out but the sound; the three give a tune the charm that I mention – a long thought and a bard's thought, and they bring the notes from the deeps of time, and the tale from the heart of the man who made it.

But not of the three best in Albainn to-day is my story, for they have not the Lost Pibroch. It is of the three best, who were not bad, in a place I ken – Half Town that stands in the wood.

You may rove for a thousand years on league-long brogues, or hurry on fairy wings from isle to isle and deep to deep, and find no equal to that same Half Town. It is not the splendour of it, nor the riches of its folk; it is not any great routh of field or sheep-fank, but the scented winds of it, and the comfort of the pine-trees round and about it on every hand. My mother used to be saying (when I had the notion of fairy tales), that once on a time, when the woods were young and thin, there was a road through them, and the pick of children of a country-side wandered among them into this place to play at sheilings. Up grew the trees, fast and tall, and shut the little folks in so that the way out they could not get if they had the mind for it. But never an out they wished for. They grew with the firs and alders, a quiet clan in the heart of the big wood, clear of the world out-by.

But now and then wanderers would come to Half Town, through the gloomy coves, under the tall trees. There were packmen with tales of the out-world. There were broken men flying from rope or hatchet. And once on a day of days came two pipers – Gilian, of Clan Lachlan of Strathlachlan, and Rory Ban, of the Macnaghtons of Dundarave. They had seen Half Town from the sea – smoking to the clear air on the hillside; and through the weary woods they came, and the dead quiet of them, and they stood on the edge of the fir-belt.

Before them was what might be a township in a dream, and to be seen at the one look, for it stood on the rising hill that goes back on Lochow.

The dogs barked, and out from the houses and in from the fields came the quiet clan to see who could be here. Biggest of all the men, one they named Coll, cried on the strangers to come forward; so out they went from the wood-edge, neither coy nor crouse, but the equal of friend or foe, and they passed the word of day.

"Hunting," they said, "in Easachosain, we found the roe come this way."

"If this way she came, she's at Duglas Water by now, so you may bide and eat. Few, indeed, come calling on us in Half Town; but whoever they are, here's the open door, and the horn spoon, and the stool by the fire."

He took them in and he fed them, nor asked their names nor calling, but when they had eaten well he said to Rory, "You have skill of the pipes; I know by the drum of your fingers on the horn spoon."

"I have tried them," said Rory, with a laugh, "a bit – a bit. My friend here is a player."

"You have the art?" asked Coll.

"Well, not what you might call the whole art," said Gilian, "but I can play – oh yes! I can play two or three ports."

"You can that!" said Rory.

"No better than yourself, Rory."

"Well, maybe not, but – anyway, not all tunes; I allow you do 'Mackay's Banner' in a pretty style."

"Pipers," said Coll, with a quick eye to a coming quarrel, "I will take you to one of your own trade in this place – Paruig Dall, who is namely for music."

"It's a name that's new to me," said Rory, short and sharp, but up they rose and followed Big Coll.

He took them to a bothy behind the Half Town, a place with turf walls and never a window, where a blind man sat winding pirns for the weaverfolks.

"This," said Coll, showing the strangers in at the door "is a piper of parts, or I'm no judge, and he has as rare a stand of great pipes as ever my eyes sat on."

"I have that same," said the blind man, with his face to the door. "Your friends, Coll?"

"Two pipers of the neighbourhood," Rory made answer. "It was for no piping we came here, but by the accident of the chase. Still and on, if pipes are here, piping there might be."

"So be it," cried Coll; "but I must go back to my cattle till night comes. Get you to the playing with Paruig Dall and I'll find you here when I come back." And with that he turned about and went off.

Paruig put down the ale and cake before the two men, and "Welcome you are," said he.

They ate the stranger's bite, and lipped the stranger's cup, and then, "Whistle 'The Macraes' March,' my fair fellow," said the blind man.

"How ken you I'm fair?" asked Rory.

"Your tongue tells that. A fair man has aye a soft bit in his speech, like the lapping of milk in a cogie; and a black one, like your friend there, has the sharp ring of a thin burn in frost running into an iron pot. 'The Macraes 'March,' *laochain.* "

Rory put a pucker on his mouth and played a little of the fine tune.

"So!" said the blind man, with his head to a side, "you had your lesson. And you, my Strathlachlan boy without beard, do you ken 'Muinntir a'Ghlinne so'?"

"How ken ye I'm Strathlachlan and beardless?" asked Gilian.

"Strathlachlan by the smell of herring-scale from your side of the house (for they told me yesterday the gannets were flying down Strathlachlan way, and that means fishing), and you have no beard I know, but in what way I know I do not know."

Gilian had the *siubhal* of the pibroch but begun when the blind man stopped him.

"You have it," he said, "you have it in a way, the Macarthur's way and that's not my way. But, no matter, let us to our piping."

The three men sat them down on three stools on the clay floor, and the blind man's pipes passed round between them.

"First," said Paruig (being the man of the house, and to get the vein of his own pipes) – "first I'll put on them 'The Vaunting.'" He stood to his shanks, a lean old man and straight, and the big drone came nigh on the black rafters. He filled the bag at a breath and swung a lover's arm round about it. To those who know not the pipes, the feel of the bag in the oxter is a gaiety lost. The sweet round curve is like a girl's waist; it is friendly and warm in the crook of the elbow and against a man's side, and to press it is to bring laughing or tears.

The bothy roared with the tuning, and then the air came melting and sweet from the chanter. Eight steps up, four to the turn, and eight down went Paruig, and the *piobaireachd* rolled to his fingers like a man's rhyming. The two men sat on the stools, with their elbows on their knees, and listened.

He played but the *urlar,* and the *crunluadh* to save time, and he played them well.

"Good indeed! Splendid, my old fellow!" cried the two; and said Gilian, "You have a way of it in the *crunluadh* not my way, but as good as ever I heard."

"It is the way of Padruig Og," said Rory. "Well I know it! There are tunes and tunes, and 'The Vaunting' is not bad in its way, but give me 'The Macraes' March.'"

He jumped to his feet and took the pipes from the old man's hands, and over his shoulder with the drones.

"Stand back, lad!" he cried to Gilian, and Gilian went nearer the door.

The march came fast to the chanter – the old tune, the fine tune that Kintail has heard before, when the wild men in their red tartan came over hill and moor; the tune with the river in it, the fast river and the courageous that kens not stop nor tarry, that runs round rock and over fall with a good humour, yet no mood for anything but the way before it. The tune of the heroes, the tune of the pinelands and the broad straths, the tune that the eagles of Loch Duich crack their beaks together when they hear, and the crows of that country-side would as soon listen to as the squeal of their babies.

"Well! mighty well!" said Paruig Dall. "You have the tartan of the clan in it."

"Not bad, I'll allow," said Gilian. "Let me try."

He put his fingers on the holes, and his heart took a leap back over two generations, and yonder was Glencoe! The grey day crawled on the white hills and the black roofs smoked below. Snow choked the pass, *eas* and corri filled with drift and flatted to the brae-face; the wind tossed quirky and cruel in the little bushes and among the smooring lintels and joists; the blood of old and young lappered on the hearthstone, and the bairn, with a knifed throat, had an icy lip on a frozen teat. Out of the place went the tramped path of the Campbell butchers – far on their way to Glenlyon and the towns of paper and ink and liars – "Muinntir a' ghlinne so, muinntir a' ghlinne so! – People, people, people of this glen, this glen, this glen!"

"Dogs! dogs! O God of grace – dogs and cowards!" cried Rory. "I could be dirking a Diarmaid or two if by luck they were near me."

"It is piping that is to be here," said Paruig, "and it is not piping for an hour nor piping for an evening, but the piping of Dunvegan that stops for sleep nor supper."

So the three stayed in the bothy and played tune about while time went by the door. The birds flew home to the branches, the long-necked beasts flapped off to the shore to spear their flat fish; the rutting deers bellowed with loud throats in the deeps of the wood that stands round Half Town, and the scents of the moist night came gusty round the door. Over the back of Auchnabreac the sun trailed his plaid of red and yellow, and the loch stretched salt and dark from Cairn Dubh to Creaggans.

In from the hill the men and the women came, weary-legged, and the bairns nodded at their heels. Sleepiness was on the land, but the pipers, piping in the bothy, kept the world awake.

"We will go to bed in good time,"said the folks, eating their suppers at their doors; "in good time when this tune is ended."But tune came on tune, and every tune better than its neighbour, and they waited.

A cruisie-light was set alowe in the blind man's bothy, and the three men played old tunes and new tunes – salute and lament and brisk dances and marches that coax tired brogues on the long roads.

"Here's 'Tulloch Ard' for you, and tell me who made it," said Rory.

'Who kens that? Here's 'Raasay's Lament,' the best port Padruig Mor ever put together."

"Tunes and tunes. I'm for 'A Kiss o'the King's Hand.'"

> "Thug mi pòg 'us pòg 'us pòg,
> Thug mi pòg do làmh an righ,
> Cha do chuir gaoth an craicionn caorach,
> Fear a fhuair an fhaoilt ach mi!"

Then a quietness came on Half Town, for the piping stopped, and the people at their doors heard but their blood thumping and the night-hags in the dark of the firwood.

"A little longer and maybe there will be more," they said to each other, and they waited; but no more music came from the drones, so they went in to bed.

There was quiet over Half Town, for the three pipers talked about the Lost Tune.

"A man my father knew," said Gilian, "heard a bit of it once in Moideart. A terrible fine tune he said it was, but sore on the mind."

"It would be the tripling," said the Macnaghton, stroking a reed with a fond hand.

"Maybe. Tripling is ill enough, but what is tripling? There is more in piping than brisk fingers. Am I not right, Paruig?"

"Right, oh! right. The Lost *Piobaireachd* asks for skilly tripling, but Macruimen himself could not get at the core of it for all his art."

"You have heard it then!" cried Gilian.

The blind man stood up and filled out his breast.

"Heard it!" he said; "I heard it, and I play it – on the *feadan*, but not on the full set. To play the tune I mention on the full set is what I have not done since I came to Half Town."

"I have ten round pieces in my sporran, and a bonnet-brooch it would take much to part me from; but they're there for the man who'll play me the Lost *Piobaireachd*," said Gilian, with the words tripping each other to the tip of his tongue.

"And here's a Macnaghton's fortune on the top of the round pieces," cried Rory, emptying his purse on the table.

The old man's face got hot and angry. "I am not," he said, "a tinker's minstrel, to give my tuning for bawbees and a quaich of ale. The king himself could not buy the tune I ken if he had but a whim for it. But when pipers ask it they can have it, and it's yours without a fee. Still if you think to learn the tune by my piping once, poor's the delusion. It is not a port to be picked up like a cockle on the sand, for it takes the schooling of years and blindness forbye."

"Blindness?"

"Blindness indeed. The thought of it is only for the dark eye."

"If we could hear it on the full set!"

"Come out, then, on the grass, and you'll hear it, if Half Town should sleep no sleep this night."

They went out of the bothy to the wet short grass. Ragged mists shook o'er Cowal, and on Ben Ime sat a horned moon like a galley of Lorn.

"I heard this tune from the Moideart man – the last in Albainn who knew it then, and he's in the clods," said the blind fellow.

He had the mouthpiece at his lip, and his hand was coaxing the bag, when a bairn's cry came from a house in the Half Town – a suckling's whimper, that, heard in the night, sets a man's mind busy on the sorrows that folks are born to. The drones clattered together on the piper's elbow and he stayed.

"I have a notion," he said to the two men. "I did not tell you that the Lost *Piobaireachd* is the *piobaireachd* of good-byes. It is the tune of broken clans, that sets the men on the foray and makes cold hearth-stones. It was played in Glenshira when Gilleasbuig Gruamach could stretch stout swordsmen from Boshang to Ben Bhuidhe, and where are the folks of Glenshira this day? I saw a cheery night in Carnus that's over Lochow, and song and story busy about the fire, and the Moideart man played it for a wager. In the morning the weans were without fathers, and Carnus men were scattered about the wide world."

"It must be the magic tune, sure enough," said Gilian.

"Magic indeed, *laochain!* It is the tune that puts men on the open road, that makes restless lads and seeking women. Here's a Half Town of dreamers and men fattening for want of men's work. They forget the world is wide and round about their fir-trees, and I can make them crave for something they cannot name."

"Good or bad, out with it," said Rory, "if you know it at all."

"Maybe no', maybe no'. I am old and done. Perhaps I have lost the right skill of the tune, for it's long since I put it on the great pipe. There's in me the strong notion to try it whatever may come of it, and here's for it."

He put his pipe up again, filled the bag at a breath, brought the booming to the drones, and then the chanter-reed cried sharp and high.

"He's on it," said Rory in Gilian's ear.

The groundwork of the tune was a drumming on the deep notes where the sorrows lie – "Come, come, come, my children, rain on the brae and the wind blowing."

"It is a salute," said Rory.

"It's the strange tune anyway," said Gilian; "listen to the time of yon!"

The tune searched through Half Town and into the gloomy pine-wood; it put an end to the whoop of the night-hag and rang to Ben Bhreac. Boatmen deep and far on the loch could hear it, and Half Town folks sat up to listen.

Its story was the story that's ill to tell – something of the heart's longing and the curious chances of life. It bound up all the tales of all the clans, and made one tale of the Gaels' past. Dirk nor sword against the tartan, but the tartan against all else, and the Gaels' target fending the hill-land and the juicy straths from the pock-pitted little black men. The winters and the summers passing fast and furious, day and night roaring in the ears, and then again the clans at variance, and warders on every pass and on every parish.

Then the tune changed.

"Folks," said the reeds, coaxing. "Wide's the world and merry the road. Here's but the old story and the women we kissed before. Come, come to the flat-lands rich and full, where the wonderful new things happen and the women's lips are still to try!"

"To-morrow," said Gilian in his friend's ear – "tomorrow I will go jaunting to the North. It has been in my mind since Beltane."

"One might be doing worse," said Rory, "and I have the notion to try a trip with my cousin to the foreign wars."

The blind piper put up his shoulder higher and rolled the air into the *crunluadh breabach* that comes prancing with variations. Pride stiffened him from heel to hip, and hip to head, and set his sinews like steel.

He was telling of the gold to get for the searching and the bucks that may be had for the hunting. "What," said the reeds, "are your poor crops, slashed by the constant rain and rotting, all for a scart in the bottom of a pot? What are your stots and heifers – black, dun, and yellow – to milch-cows and horses? Here's but the same for ever – toil and sleep, sleep and toil even on, no feud nor foray nor castles to harry – only the starved field and the sleeping moss. Let us to a brisker place! Over yonder are the long straths and the deep rivers and townships strewn thick as your corn-rigs; over yonder's the place of the packmen's tales and the packmen's wares: steep we the withies and go!"

The two men stood with heads full of bravery and dreaming – men in a carouse. "This," said they, "is the notion we had, but had no words for. It's a poor trade piping and eating and making amusement when one might be wandering up and down the world. We must be packing the haversacks."

Then the *crunluadh mach* came fast and furious on the chanter, and Half Town shook with it. It buzzed in the ear like the flowers in the Honey Croft, and made commotion among the birds rocking on their eggs in the wood.

"*So! so!*" barked the *iolair* on Craig-an-eas. "I have heard before it was an ill thing to be satisfied; in the morning I'll try the kids on Maam-side, for the hares here are wersh and tough." "Hearken, dear," said the *lon-dubh*. "I know now why my beak is gold; it is because I once ate richer berries than the whortle, and in season I'll look for them on the braes of Glenfinne." "Honk-unk," said the fox, the cunning red fellow, "am not I the fool to be staying on this little brae when I know so many roads elsewhere?"

And the people sitting up in their beds in Half Town moaned for something new. "Paruig Dall is putting the strange tune on her there," said they. "What the meaning of it is we must ask in the morning, but, *ochanoch!* it leaves one hungry at the heart." And then gusty winds came snell from the north, and where the dark crept first, the day made his first showing, so that Ben Ime rose black against a grey sky.

"That's the Lost *Piobaireachd*," said Paruig Dall when the bag sunk on his arm.

And the two men looked at him in a daze.

Sometimes in the spring of the year the winds from Lorn have it their own way with the Highlands. They will come tearing furious over the hundred hills, spurred the faster by the prongs of Cruachan and Dunchuach, and the large woods of home toss before them like corn before the hook. Up come the poor roots and over on their broken arms go the tall trees, and in the morning the deer will trot through new lanes cut in the forest.

A wind of that sort came on the full of the day when the two pipers were leaving Half Town.

"Stay till the storm is over," said the kind folks; and "Your bed and board are here for the pipers forty days," said Paruig Dall. But "No" said the two; "we have business that your *piobaireachd* put us in mind of."

"I'm hoping that I did not play yon with too much skill," said the old man.

"Skill or no skill," said Gilian, "the like of yon I never heard. You played a port that makes poor enough all ports ever one listened to, and piping's no more for us wanderers."

"Blessings with thee!" said the folks all, and the two men went down into the black wood among the cracking trees.

Six lads looked after them, and one said, "It is an ill day for a body to take the world for his pillow, but what say you to following the pipers?"

"It might," said one, "be the beginning of fortune. I am weary enough of this poor place, with nothing about it but wood and water and tufty grass. If we went now there might be gold and girls at the other end."

They took crooks and bonnets and went after the two pipers. And when they were gone half a day, six women said to their men, "Where can the lads be?"

"We do not know that," said the men, with hot faces, "but we might be looking." They kissed their children and went, with *cromags* in their hands, and the road they took was the road the King of Errin rides, and that is the road to the end of days.

A weary season fell on Half Town, and the very bairns dwined at the breast for a change of fortune. The women lost their strength, and said, "To-day my back is weak, tomorrow I will put things to right," and they looked slack-mouthed and heedless-eyed at the sun wheeling round the trees. Every week a man or two would go to seek something – a lost heifer or a wounded roe that was never brought back – and a new trade came to the place, the selling of herds. Far away in the low country, where the winds are warm and the poorest have money, black cattle were wanted, so the men of Half Town made up long droves and took them round Glen Beag and the Rest.

Wherever they went they stayed, or the clans on the roadside put them to steel, for Half Town saw them no more. And a day came when all that was left in that fine place were but women and children and a blind piper.

"Am I the only man here?" asked Paruig Dall when it came to the bit, and they told him he was.

"Then here's another for fortune!" said he, and he went down through the woods with his pipes in his oxter.

Red Hand

THE smell of wet larch was in the air, and Glenaora was aburst to the coaxing of Spring. Paruig Dall the piper – son of the son of Iain Mor – filled his broad chest with two men's wind, and flung the drones over his shoulder. They dangled a little till the bag swelled out, and the first blast rang in the ear of the morning. Rough and noisy, the reeds cried each other down till a master's hand held them in check, and the long soft singing of the *piobaireachd* floated out among the tartan ribbons. The grey peak of Drimfern heard the music; the rock that wards the mouth of Carnus let it pass through the gap and over the hill and down to the isles below; Dun Corrbhile and Dunchuach, proud Kilmune, the Paps of Salachary, and a hundred other braes around, leaned over to listen to the vaunting notes that filled the valley. "The Glen, the Glen is mine!" sang the blithe chanter; and, by Finne's sword, Macruimen himself could not have fingered it better!

It was before Paruig Dall left for Half Town; before the wars that scorched the glens; and Clan Campbell could cock its bonnet in the face of all Albainn. Paruig was old, and Paruig was blind, as the name of him tells, but he swung with a king's port up and down on the short grass, his foot firm to every beat of the tune, his kilt tossing from side to side like a bard's song, his sporran leaping gaily on his brown knees. Two score of lilting steps to the burnside, a slow wheel on a brogue-heel, and then back with the sun-glint on the buckles of his belt.

The men, tossing the caber and hurling the *clachneart* against the sun beyond the peat-bog, paused in their stride at the chanter's boast, jerked the tartan tight on their loins, and came over to listen; the women, posting blankets for the coming sheiling, stopped their splashing in the little linn, and hummed in a dream; and men and women had mind of the days that were, when the Glen was soft with the blood of men, for the Stewarts were over the way from Appin.

"God's splendour! but he can play too," said the piper's son, with his head areel to the fine tripling.

Then Paruig pushed the bag further into his oxter, and the tune changed. He laid the ground of "Bodaich nam Briogais," and such as knew the story saw the "carles with the breeks" broken and flying before Glenurchy's thirsty swords, far north of Morven, long days of weary march

10

through spoiled glens.

"It's fine playing, I'll allow," said the blind man's son, standing below a saugh-tree with the bag of his bannered pipes in the crook of his arm. He wore the dull tartan of the Diarmaids, and he had a sprig of gall in his bonnet, for he was in Black Duncan's tail. "Son of Paruig Dall," said the Chief seven years ago come Martinmas, "if you're to play like your father, there's but Dunvegan for you, and the schooling of Patrick Macruimen." So Tearlach went to Skye – cold isle of knives and caves – and in the college of Macruimen he learned the *piob-mhor*. Morning and evening, and all day between, he fingered the *feadan* or the full set – gathering and march, massacre and moaning, and the stately salute. Where the lusty breeze comes in salt from Vaternish across Loch Vegan, and the purple loom of Uist breaks the sunset's golden bars, he stood on the braes over against Borearaig and charmed the grumbling tide. And there came a day that he played "The Lament of the Harp-Tree" with the old years of sturdy fight and strong men all in the strain of it, and Patrick Macruimen said, "No more, lad; go home: Lochow never heard another like you." As a cock with its comb uncut, came the stripling from Skye.

"Father," he had said, "you play not ill for a blind man, but you miss the look on the men's faces, and that's half the music. Forbye, you are old, and your fingers are slow on the grace-notes. Here's your own flesh and blood can show you fingering there was never the like of anywhere east the Isles."

The stepmother heard the brag. "*A pheasain!*" she snapped, with hate in her peat-smoked face. "Your father's a man, and you are but a boy with no heart for a long day. A place in Black Duncan's tail, with a gillie to carry your pipes and knapsack, is not, mind ye, all that's to the making of a piper."

Tearlach laughed in her face. "Boy or man," said he, "look at me! north, east, south, and west, where is the one to beat me? Macruimen has the name, but there were pipers before Macruimen, and pipers will come after him."

"It's maybe as you say," said Paruig. "The stuff's in you, and what is in must out; but give me *cothrom na Feinne,* and old as I am, with Finne's chance, and that's fair play, I can maybe make you crow less crouse. Are ye for trying?"

"I am at the training of a new chanter-reed," said Tearlach; "but let it be when you will."

They fixed a day, and went out to play against each other for glory, and so it befell that on this day Paruig Dall was playing "The Glen is Mine" and "Bodaich nam Briogais" in a way to make stounding hearts.

Giorsal snapped her fingers in her stepson's face when her husband closed the *crunluadh* of his *piobaireachd*.

"Can you better it, bastard?" snarled she.

"Here goes for it, whatever!" said Tearlach, and over his back went the banner with its boar's head sewn on gold. A pretty lad, by the cross! clean-cut of limb and light of foot, supple of loin, with the toss of the shoulder that never a decent piper lacked. The women who had been at the linn leaned on each other all in the soft larch-scented day, and looked at him out of deep eyes; the men on the heather arose and stood nigher.

A little tuning, and then

> "Is comadh leam's comadh leam, cogadh na sithe,
> Marbhar 'sa chogadh na crochar 's an t-sith mi."

"Peace or war!" cried Giorsal, choking in anger, to her man – "peace or war! the black braggart! it's an asp ye have for a son, goodman!"

The lad's fingers danced merry on the chanter, and the shiver of something to come fell on all the folk around.

The old hills sported with the prancing tune; Dun Corrbhile tossed it to Drimfern, and Drimfern sent it leaping across the flats of Kilmune to the green corries of Lecknamban. "Love, love, the old tune; come and get flesh!" rasped a crow to his mate far off on misty Ben Bhreac, and the heavy black wings flapped east. The friendly wind forgot to dally with the pine-tuft and the twanging bog-myrtle, the plash of Aora in its brown linn was the tinkle of wine in a goblet. "Peace or war, peace or war; come which will, we care not," sang the pipe-reeds, and there was the muster and the march, hot-foot rush over the rotting rain-wet moor, the jingle of iron, the dunt of pike and targe, the choked roar of hate and hunger, batter and slash and fall, and behind, the old, old feud with Appin!

Leaning forward, lost in a dream, stood the swank lads of Aora. They felt at their hips, where were only empty belts, and one said to his child, "White love, get me yon long knife with the nicks on it, and the basket-hand, for I am sick of shepherding." The bairn took a look at his face and went home crying.

And the music still poured on. 'Twas "I got a Kiss o' the King's Hand" and "The Pretty Dirk," and every air better than another. The fairy pipe of the Wee Folk's Knowe never made a sweeter fever of sound, yet it hurt the ears of the women, who had reason to know the payment of pipers' springs.

"Stop, stop, O Tearlach og!" they cried; "enough of war: have ye not a reel in your budget?"

"There was never a reel in Boreraig," said the lad, and he into "Duniveg's Warning," the tune Coll Ciotach heard his piper play in the west on a day when a black bitch from Dunstaffnage lay panting for him, and his barge put nose about in time to save his skin.

"There's the very word itself in it," said Paruig, forgetting the taunting of Giorsal and all but a father's pride.

'Twas in the middle of the "Warning" Black Duncan, his toe on the stirrup, came up from Castle Inneraora, with a gillie-wet-foot behind, on his way to Lochow.

"It's down yonder you should be, Sir Piper, and not blasting here for drink," said he, switching his trews with his whip and scowling under black brows at the people. "My wife is sick of the *clarsach* and wants the pipes."

"I'm no woman's piper, Lochow; your wife can listen to the hum of her spinning-wheel if she's weary of her harp," said the lad; and away rode the Chief, and back to the linn went the women, and the men to the *cabar* and the stone, and Tearlach, with an extra feather in his bonnet, home to Inneraora, leaving a gibe as he went, for his father.

Paruig Dall cursed till the evening at the son he never saw, and his wife poisoned his mind.

"The Glen laughs at you, man, from Carnus to Croitbhile. It's a black, burning day of shame for you, Paruig Dall!"

"Lord, it's a black enough day for me at the best!" said the blind man.

"It's disgraced by your own ill-got son you are, by a boy with no blood on his *biodag*, and the pride to crow over you."

And Paruig cursed anew, by the Cross and the Dogs of Lorn, and the White Glaive of Light the giants wear, and the Seven Witches of Cothmar. He was bad though he was blind, and he went back to the start of time for his language "But *Dhé!* the boy can play!" he said at the last.

"Oh, *amadain dhoill!*" cried the woman; "if it was I, a claw was off the cub before the mouth of day."

"Witless woman, men have played the pipes before now, lacking a finger: look at Alasdair Corrag!"

"Allowing; but a hand's as easy to cut as a finger for a man who has gralloched deer with a keen *sgian-dubh*. Will ye do't or no'?"

Paruig would hearken no more, and took to his pillow.

Rain came with the gloaming. Aora, the splendid river roared up the dark glen from the Salmon Leap; the hills gathered thick and heavy round about the scattered townships, the green new tips of fir and the copper leaves of the young oaks moaned in the wind. Then salt airs came tearing up from the sea, grinding branch on branch, and the whole land smoked with the drumming of rain that slanted on it hot and fast.

Giorsal arose, her clothes still on her, put a plaid on her black head, and the thick door banged back on the bed as she dived into the storm. Her heavy feet sogged through the boggy grass, the heather clutched at her draggled coat-tails to make her stay, but she filled her heart with one thought, and that was hate, and behold! she was on the slope of the Black Bull before her blind husband guessed her meaning. Castle Inneraora lay at the foot of the woody dun, dozing to the music of the salt loch that made tumult and spume north and south in the hollow of the mountains. Now and then the moon took a look at things, now and then a night-hag in the dripping wood hooted as the rain whipped her breast feathers; a roe leaped out of the gloom and into it with a feared hoof-plunge above Carlonan; a thunderbolt struck in the dark against the brow of Ben Ime and rocked the world.

In the cold hour before the mouth of day the woman was in the piper's room at the gate of Inneraora, where never a door was barred against the night while Strong Colin the warder could see from the Fort of Dunchuach to Cladich. Tearlach the piper lay on his back, with the glow of a half-dead peat on his face and hands. "Paruig, Paruig!" said the woman to herself, as she softly tramped out the peat-fire and turned to the bed. And lo! it was over. Her husband's little black knife made a fast sweep on the sleeper's wrist, and her hand was drenched with the hot blood of her husband's son.

Tearlach leaped up with a roar in the dark and felt for his foe; but the house was empty, for Giorsal was running like a hind across the soaked stretch of Cairnban. The lightning struck at Glenaora in jagged fury and confusion; the thunder drummed hollow on Creag Dubh: in a turn of the pass at the Three Bridges the woman met her husband.

"Daughter of hell!" said he, "is't done? and was't death?"

"Darling," said she, with a fond laugh, "'twas only a brat's hand. You can give us 'The Glen is Mine!' in the morning."

The Secret of the Heather-Ale

DOWN Glenaora threescore and ten of Diarmaid's stout fellows took the road on a fine day. They were men from Carnus, with more of Clan Artair than Campbell in them; but they wore Gilleasbuig Gruamach's tartan, and if they were not on Gilleasbuig Gruamach's errand, it makes little difference on our story. It was about the time Antrim and his dirty Irishers came scouring through our glens with flambeaux, dirk and sword and other arms invasive, and the country was back at its old trade of fighting, with not a sheiling from end to end, except on the slopes of Shira Glen, where a clan kept free of battle and drank the finest of heather-ale that the world envied the secret of.

"Lift we and go, for the Cattle's before!" said Alasdair Piobaire on the chanter of a Dunvegan great-pipe – a neat tune that roared gallant and far from Carnus to Baracaldine; so there they were, the pick of swank fellows on the road!

At the head of them was Niall Mor a' Chamais – the same gentleman namely in story for many an art and the slaughter of the strongest man in the world, as you'll find in the writings of my Lord Archie. "God! look at us!" said he, when his lads came over the hill in the grey mouth of day. "Are not we the splendid men? Fleas will there be this day in the hose of the Glenshira folk." And he sent his targe in the air in a bravado, catching it by the prong in its navel, smart and clean, when it whirled back.

Hawks yelped as they passed; far up on Tullich there was barking of eagles; the brogues met the road as light as the stag-slot; laughing, singing, roaring; sword-heads and pikes dunting on wooden targets – and only once they looked back at their women high on the brae-face.

The nuts were thick on the roadside, hanging heavy from swinging branches, and some of the men pulled them off as they passed, stayed for more, straggled, and sang bits of rough songs they ken over many of on Lochowside to this day. So Niall Mor glunched at his corps from under his bonnet and showed his teeth.

"Gather in, gather in," said he; "ye march like a drove of low-country cattle. Alasdair, put 'Baile Inneraora' on her!"

Alasdair changed his tune, and the good march of Clan Diarmaid went swinging down the glen.

The time passed; the sun stood high and hot; clucking from the fir-plantings came woodcock and cailzie; the two rivers were crossed, and the Diarmaids slockened their thirst at the water of Altan Aluinn, whose birth is somewhere in the bogs beside tall Bhuidhe Ben.

Where the clans met was at the Foal's Gap, past Maam. A score of the MacKellars ran out in a line from the bushes, and stotted back from the solid weight of Diarmaid moving in a lump and close-shouldered in the style Niall Mor got from the Italian soldier. Some fell, hacked on the head by the heavy slash of the dry sword; some gripped too late at the pikes that kittled them cruelly; and one – Iver-of-the-Oars – tripped on a root of heather, and fell with his breast on the point of a Diarmaid's dirk.

To the hills went a fast summons, and soon at the mouth of the gap came twoscore of the MacKellars. They took a new plan, and close together faced the green tartan, keeping it back at the point of steel, though the pick of Glenaora wore it, and the brogues slipped on the brae-face. It was fast cut and drive, quick flash of the dirk, with the palm up and the hand low to find the groin, and a long reach with the short black knife. The choked breath hissed at teeth and nose, the salt smell of new blood brought a shiver to birch-leaf and gall. But ever the green tartan had the best of it.

"Bas, bas, Dhiarmaid!" cried Calum Dubh, coming up on the back of his breaking two-score with fresh lads from Elerigmor, bed-naked to the hide, and a new fury fell on the two clans tearing at it in the narrow hollow in between the rocky hills. So close they were, there was small room for the whirl of the basket-hilt, and "Mind Tom-a-Phubaill and the shortened steel!" cried Niall Mor, smashing a pretty man's face with a blow from the iron guard of his Ferrara sword. The halberts, snapped at the haft to make whittles, hammered on the target-hides like stones on a coffin, or rang on the bosses; the tartan ripped when the stuck one rolled on his side before the steel could be twisted out; below the foot the grass felt warm and greasy, and the reason was not ill to seek.

Once it looked like the last of Calum Dubh. He was facing Niall Mor, sword and targe, and Niall Mor changed the sword to the other hand, pulled the *sgian-dubh* from his garter, and with snapping teeth pushed like a lightning fork below MacKellar's target. An Elerigmor man ran in between; the little black knife sunk into his belly with a moist plunge, and the blood spouted on the deer-horn haft.

"Mallachd ort! I meant yon for a better man," cried Niall Mor; "but it's well as it is, for the secret's to the fore," and he stood up dour and tall against a new front of MacKellar's men.

Then the sky changed, and a thin smirr of warm rains fell on the glen like smoke; some black-cattle bellowed at the ford in a wonder at where their herds could be, and the herds – stuck, slashed, and cudgelled – lay stiffening on the torn grass between the gap and MacKellar's house. From end to end of the glen there was no man left but was at the fighting. The hook was tossed among the corn; the man hot-foot behind the roe, turned when he had his knife at its throat, to go to war; a lover left his lass among the heather; and all, with tightened belts, were at the old game with Clan Diarmaid, while their women, far up on the sappy levels between the hill-tops and beside the moor-lochs, span at the wheel or carded wool, singing songs with light hearts and thinking no danger.

Back went MacKellar's men before Niall Mor and his sturdy lads from Carnus, the breeder of soldiers – back through the gap and down on the brae to the walls of Calum Dubh.

"*Illean, 'illean!*" cried Calum; "lads, lads! they have us, sure enough. Oh! pigs and thieves! squint mouths and sons of liars!"

The cry gathered up the strength of all that was left of his clan, Art and Uileam, the Maam lads, the brothers from Drimlea and two from over Stron hill, and they stood up together against the Carnus men – a gallant madness! They died fast and hard, and soon but Calum and his two sons were left fencing, till a rush of Diarmaids sent them through the door of the house and tossed among the peats.

"Give in and your lives are your own," said Niall Mor, wiping his sword on his shirt-sleeve, and with all that were left of his Diarmaids behind his back.

To their feet stood the three MacKellars. Calum looked at the folk in front of him, and had mind of other ends to battles. "To die in a house like a rat were no great credit," said he, and he threw his sword on the floor, where the blades of Art and Uileam soon joined it.

With tied arms the father and his sons were taken outside, where the air was full of the scents of birch and gall new-washed. The glen, clearing fast of mist, lay green and sweet for mile and mile, and far at its mouth the fat Blaranbuie woods chuckled in the sun.

"I have you now," said Niall Mor. "Ye ken what we seek. It's the old ploy – the secret of the ale."

Calum laughed in his face, and the two sons said things that cut like knives.

"Man! I'm feared ye'll rue this," said Niall Mor, calm enough. "Ye may laugh, but – what would ye call a gentleman's death?"

"With the sword or the dagger in the hand, and a Diarmaid or two before me," cried Calum.

"Well, there might be worse ways of travelling yont – indeed there could ill be better; but if the secret of the ale is not to be ours for the asking, ye'll die a less well-bred death."

"Name it, man, name it," said Calum. "Might it be tow at the throat and a fir-branch."

"Troth," said Niall Mor, "and that were too gentle a travelling. The

Scaurnoch's on our way, and the crows at the foot of it might relish a Glen Shira carcass."

Uileam whitened at the notion of so ugly an end, but Calum only said, "Die we must any way," and Art whistled a bit of a pipe-tune, grinding his heel on the moss.

Niall Mor made to strike the father on the face, but stayed his hand and ordered the three in-by, with a few of his corps to guard them. Up and down Glen Shira went the Diarmaids, seeking the brewing-cave, giving hut and home to the flame, and making black hearths and low lintels for the women away in the sheilings. They buried their dead at Kilblaan, and, with no secret the better, set out for Scaurnoch with Calum and his sons.

The MacKellars were before, like a *spreidh of* stolen cattle, and the lot of the driven herd was theirs. They were laughed at and spat on, and dirk-hilts and *cromags* hammered on their shoulders, and through Blaranbuie wood they went to the bosky elbow of Dun Corrbhile and round to the Dun beyond.

Calum, for all his weariness, stepped like a man with a lifetime's plans before his mind; Art looked about him in the fashion of one with an eye to woodcraft; Uileam slouched with a heavy foot, white at the jaw and wild of eye.

The wood opened, the hunting-road bent about the hill-face to give a level that the eye might catch the country spread below. Loch Finne stretched far, from Ardno to French Foreland, a glassy field, specked with one sail off Creaggans. When the company came to a stand, Calum Dubh tossed his head to send the hair from his eyes, and looked at what lay below. The Scaurnoch broke at his feet, the grey rock-face falling to a depth so deep that weary mists still hung upon the sides, jagged here and there by the top of a fir-tree. The sun, behind the Dun, gave the last of her glory to the Cowal Hills; Hell's Glen filled with wheeling mists; Ben Ime, Ben Vane, and Ben Arthur crept together and held princely converse on the other side of the sea.

All in a daze of weariness and thinking the Diarmaids stood, and looked and listened, and the curlews were crying bitter on the shore.

"Oh, haste ye, lads, or it's not Carnus for us to-night," cried Niall Mor. "We have business before us, and long's the march to follow. The secret, black fellow!"

Calum Dubh laughed, and spat in a bravado over the edge of the rock.

"Come, fool, if we have not the word from you before the sun's off Sithean Sluaidhe, your sleep this night is yonder," and he pointed at the pit below.

Calum laughed the more. "If it was hell itself," said he, "I would not save my soul from it."

"Look, man, look! the Sithean Sluaidhe's getting black, and any one of ye can save the three yet. I swear it on the cross of my knife."

Behind the brothers, one, John-Without-Asking, stood, with a gash on his face, eager to give them to the crows below.

A shiver came to Uileam's lips; he looked at his father with a questioning face, and then stepped back a bit from the edge, making to speak to the tall man of Chamis.

Calum saw the meaning, and spoke fast and thick.

"Stop, stop," said he; "it's a trifle of a secret, after all, and to save life ye can have it."

Art took but a little look at his father's face, then turned round on Shira Glen and looked on the hills where the hunting had many a time been sweet. "Maam no more," said he to himself; "but here's death in the hero's style!"

"I thought you would tell it," laughed Niall Mor. "There was never one of your clan but had a tight grip of his little life."

"Ay!" said Calum Dubh; "but it's *my* secret. I had it from one who made me swear on the holy steel to keep it; but take me to Carnus, and I'll make you the heather-ale."

"So be't, and – "

"But there's this in it, I can look no clansmen nor kin in the face after telling it, so Art and Uileam must be out of the way first."

"Death, MacKellar?"

"That same."

Uileam shook like a leaf, and Art laughed, with his face still to Shira, for he had guessed his father's mind.

"Faith!" said Niall Mor, "and that's an easy thing enough," and he nodded to John-Without-Asking.

The man made stay nor tarry. He put a hand on each son's back and pushed them over the edge to their death below. One cry came up to the listening Diarmaids, one cry and no more – the last gasp of a craven.

"Now we'll take you to Carnus, and you'll make us the ale, the fine ale, the cream of rich heather-ale," said Niall Mor putting a knife to the thongs that tied MacKellar's arms to his side.

With a laugh and a fast leap Calum Dubh stood back on the edge of the rock again.

"Crook-mouths, fools, pigs' sons! did ye think it?" he cried. "Come with me and my sons and ye'll get ale, ay, and death's black wine, at the foot of Scaurnoch." He caught fast and firm at John-Without-Asking, and threw himself over the rock-face. They fell as the scart dives, straight to the dim sea of mist and pine-tip, and the Diarmaids threw themselves on their breasts to look over. There was nothing to see of life but the crows swinging on black feathers; there was nothing to hear but the crows scolding.

Niall Mor put the bonnet on his head and said his first and last friendly thing of a foe.

"Yon," said he, "had the heart of a man!"

Boboon's Children

FROM Knapdale to Lorn three wandering clans share the country between them, and of the three the oldest and the greatest are the swart Macdonalds, children of the Old Boboon.

You will come on them on Wade's roads, – jaunty fellows, a bit dour in the look, and braggart; or girls with sloe-eyes, tall and supple, not with a flat slouching foot on the soil, but high in the instep, bounding and stag-sure. At their head will be a long lean old man on crutches – John Fine Macdonald – Old Boboon, the father and head of the noblest of wander-ing tribes.

"Sir," will Boboon say to you, "I am the fellow you read of in books as the teller of Fingalian tales; wilt hear one of them for a poor Saxon shilling, or wilt buy my lures for the fish? Or perhaps a display of scholarly piping by my daughter's son – the gallant scamp! – who has carried arms for his king?"

If one must have the truth, the piping is bad piping, but the fish-lures and the tales are the best in the world. You will find some of the tales in the writings of Iain Og of Isla – such as "The Brown Bear of the Green Glen"; but the best are to hear as Boboon minds them when he sits with you on the roadside or on the heather beside the evening fire, when the brown fluffy eagles bark at the mist on Braevallach. Listen well to them, for this person has the gift. He had it from his father, who had it from *his* father, who had it from a mother, who, in deep trouble and disease, lay awake through long nights gathering thoughts as healthy folks gather nuts – a sweet thing enough from a sour husk.

And if time were your property (as it should be the portion of every wiselike man), you might hear many tales from Old Boboon, but never the tale of his own three chances.

It happened once upon a time that the captain in the town took a notion to make Boboon into a tame house-man instead of a creature of the woods and highways. He took him first by himself and clapped him into a kilt of his own tartan eight yards round the buttocks, full pleated, with hose of fine worsted, and a coat with silver buttons. He put a pickle money in his sporran, and gave him a place a little way down his table. The feeding was high and the work was to a wanderer's fancy; for it was but whistling to a dog now and then, chanting a stave, or telling a story, or roaming through the garden behind the house.

"Ho, ho!" said Boboon, "am not I the sturdy fellow come to his own?" and about the place he would go with a piper's swagger, switching the grass and shrubs with a withie as he went, in the way gentlemen use riding-sticks.

But when Inneraora town lay in the dark of the winter night, and the captain's household slept, Boboon would hear his clan calling on him outside the wall.

"Boboon! oh, Boboon! old hero! come and collogue with your children."

He would go to the wall, which was lower on the inside than the out (and is, indeed, the wall of old Quinten, where a corps of Campbells, slaughtered by Inverlochy dogs, lie under a Latin stone), and he would look down at his friends running about like polecats in the darkness, in their ragged kilts and trews, their stringy hair tossing in the wind. The women themselves would be there, with the bairns whining on their backs.

"Ay! ay! this is you, my hearty folk!" he would say; "glad am I to see you and smell the wood-fire reek off you. How is it on the road?"

"From here we have not moved since you left us, John Fine. We are camped in the Blue Quarry, and you never came near your children and friends."

"God! and here's the one that's sorry for that same. But over the walls they will not let me. 'If gentleman you would be,' says the captain, 'you must keep out of woods and off the highway.'"

"And you like it, Boboon?"

"Like it, heroes! But for the honour and ease of it, give me a fir-root fire in Glen Croe and a dinner of *fuarag*. It is not the day so much as the night. Lying in-by there on a posted-bed, I choke for the want of air, though the windows and doors are open wide."

"Come away with us, Boboon; we have little luck with the fish, and few are our stories since you took to the town."

"No, no, dears. Conan's curse, and I tell you no! In this place there is comfort, and every day its own bellyful."

"But the freedom out-by, John, old hero! Last night we had the bravest of fires; the sparks flew like birds among the Duke's birches, the ground was snug and dry, and – "

"Begone! I tell ye no!"

"Listen! To-day we were among the white hares beyond the Beannan, thwacking the big fat fellows with our clubs. Such sport was not in all Albainn!"

"White hares!"

"White hares, old John! And Alasdair Beag has some new tunes since you left us – a *piobaireachd* he picked up from a Mull man."

"Would it be 'Failte an Roich'?"

"Better than that by far; a masterly tune! Come out and hear him."

But Old Boboon leaned with his arms on the wall and made no move to be off with his children.

"Come and stravaig," said the girls, and his daughter Betty put a foot in a cranny and pulled herself up beside him to put coaxing arms round his neck.

"Calf of my heart!" said Boboon, stroking her hair, soft handed.

"We have the fine feeding," said the girl in his ear. "Yesterday it was plotted trout in the morning and tunnag's eggs; dinner was a collop off a fat hind."

"A gralloched hind?"

"No, nor gralloched! That is a fool's fashion and the spoiling of good meat. But come with us, father. Think of the burns bubbling, and the stars through the branches, and the fresh airs of the morning!"

"Down, down, you bitch! Would ye tempt me?" cried Boboon, pushing the girl from the wall and hurrying back with shaking knees to the Latin stone. The night was deep black, and for all he could tell by eyesight, he might have been in the middle of breezy Moor Rannoch, but the town gables crowded thick and solid round his heart. He missed the free flowing winds; there was a smell of peat and coal from dead house-fires, and he spat the dust of lime from his throat.

Over the wall the clan scraped and skurried as weasels do. They dared make no noise for fear the town should waken, but in hoarse voices they called all together –

"Boboon, Boboon, oh! come home to the wood, Boboon!"

"Am not I the poor caged one?" said Boboon to himself, and he ran in that he might hear no more.

It was the same the next night and the next, and it looked like going on without end. Ever the wanderers coming at night to the wall and craving their head to come out. And one night they threw over a winged black-cock that fell with beating feathers at Boboon's feet as he stood in the dark listening to the swart Macdonalds whining out-by.

He picked up the bird and ran kind fingers through its feathers. The heat coursed in its breast and burned to a fever in its wounded oxter. Its little heart beat on Boboon's thumb like a drumstick.

"Poor bird!" said he; "well I ken where ye came from, and the merry times ye had. Ye hatched in the braes of Ben Bhuidhe, and clucked on the reedy places round about the side of that tall hill. Before your keen eyes in the morning was the Dubh Loch, and the Shira – winding like a silver belt. Sure am I ye took wing for it with the day, and over Stuc Scardan to Aora Glen to make merry among your mates in the heather and the fern. Oh! *choillich-dhuibh, choillich-dhuibh,* hard's our fate with broken wings and the heart still strong!"

He thrawed the bird's neck, and then went over the wall to join his clan.

His second chance ended no better. He was back in a new kilt and jacket a twelvemonth later, and this time the captain tried the trick of a dog's freedom – out on the road as he liked by day, but kennel at night.

One day Boboon was on his master's errand round Stron. It was the spring of the year. The shore, at the half-ebb, was clean and sweet, and the tide lapped at the edge as soft as a cat at milk.

Going round Stron on the hard yellow road, he got to think of the sea's good fortune, – of the many bays it wandered into by night or day; of its friendship with far-out forelands, and its brisk quarrels with the black rocks. Here was no dyke at any time, but all freedom, the restlessness and the roaming, sleep or song as the mood had it, and the ploys with galleys and gabberts; the cheery halloo of the winds and the waving of branches on foreign isles to welcome one.

The road opened before him in short swatches – the sort of road a wanderer likes, with not too much of it to be seen at one look. In the hazelwood by the way the bark of the young trees glistened like brass; thin new switches shot out straight as shelisters. John Fine, with the sun heating his back, started at the singing of Donnacha Ban's "Coire Cheathaich": –

> "O 'twas gladsome to go a-hunting
>   Out in the dew of the sunny morn!
> For the great red stag was never wanting,
>   Nor the fawn, nor the doe with never a horn.
>
> My beauteous corri, my misty corri!
>   What light feet trod thee in joy and pride!
> What strong hand gathered thy precious treasures,
>   What great hearts leaped on thy craggy side!"

Rounding Dundarave, the road lay straight before him till it thinned in the distance to a needle-point pricking the trees, and at the end of it was a cloud of dust.

"What have I here?" said Boboon to himself, stretching out with long steps, the kilt flapping against the back of his knees.

The cloud came close, and lo! here was his own clan on the march, draggled and stoury, rambling, scattered like crows, along the road.

"Boboon! Boboon!" they cried, and they hung about him, fingering his fine clothes.

He looked at their brown flesh, he saw the yellow soil in the crannies of their brogues, the men loose and blackguardly, the women red-cheeked, ripe, and big-breasted, with bold eyes, and all had enchantment for him! A stir set up in his heart that he could not put down.

"Where were you yesterday?" he asked.

"On the side of the Rest in Glen Croe, with dry beds of white hay and no hurry."

"Where are you for?"

"Have you forgotten the wanderer's ways, Boboon? Where does this road go to?"

"Well ye ken, my heroes! It goes to the end of a man's will. If the man says, 'I bide here,' it's the end of the road; but if he has the notion, it will take him to the end of days. That, by my soul! is the charm of all roads that are not in towns; and now that I think of it, let the captain whistle on his errand, for I'm Boboon and sick of the causey stones."

So night found Boboon and his clan far in at the back of Auchnabreac, town-muir and bonny place, where some we ken would sooner be than wandering o'er the world.

And the days passed, and at Martinmas the captain was at Kilmichael Market, and he came on Boboon with his people on the edge of the market-place. Boboon in those days was as straight as a young saugh-wand, sharp and thin, all thong at the joints, and as supple as a wild cat. He was giving a display with the *sgian-dubh*, stabbing it on the ground at the back of his left heel and twisting his right arm round the leg to get the blade out of the ground without bending the knee. It was a trick to take the eye, but neither bardic nor soldierly, yet there was a throng of drovers about him. Along with him was his daughter Betty, who took after him for looks, but had her dead mother's dainty tongue, and from her mother a little book-schooling John Fine had never the need of.

The eye of the captain fell on the two of them as they stood there, with their forty clan-folk going about the market, and he was gripped by a new notion to give Boboon the third and the last chance.

"Boboon!" he said, "come back to the town this once, and I'll put you and your daughter up together in a house of your own."

Before a week was out the thing was as he wanted. Boboon and Betty got a room in Macvicar's Land, with a wooden floor, and a fire on the side of the wall with a built-in chimney, and other gentilities beside. They stayed for months, and they stayed for years, and the clan craved them in vain to come home. Betty was put to the books and the arts of ladydom by the captain's mother and sister, and she took to them like a Ridir's daughter. She lost the twang of the road-folk; she put her errant hair in leash; she grew to the habit of snodding and redding, until for grace and good looks she was the match of them that taught her.

One day the captain, walking in his garden in deep cogitation, fell in the way of the girl as she roamed among the bushes. He got for the first time the true glance of her (for one may look at a person for years and not see the reality till a scale falls from the eyes), and behold! here was a woman who set his heart drumming.

It was that very night Boboon put an end to his last chance.

The strong sun of the day left the night hot and clammy, and a haze hung on the country such as one sees in these parts in keenest frost. Macvicar's Land was full of smells – of sweating flesh and dirty water, of fish and the rotting airs of sunless holes – and the dainty nose of Macdonald took a disgust. He flung open door and window, and leaned out at the window with his neck bared and his mouth stretched wide gasping to the air. The bairns in the back-land looked up and laughed.

"Look at Boboon, Boboon, Boboon, the father of Lady Betty!" they cried, and John Fine shook his fist and cursed their families.

But there was no ease from the trouble in this fashion, so he got up and went behind the town, and threw himself under the large trees with an ear to the ground. Beside him the cattle crunched the sappy grass in so sweet and hearty mouthfuls that he could well wish he had the taste of nature himself, and they breathed great breaths of content. His keen ears could catch the hopping of beasts on the grass and the scratching of claws in the wood, he could hear the patter of little feet, and the birds above him scraping on the bark when they turned in their sleep. A townman would think the world slept, so great was the booming of quietness; but Boboon heard the song of the night, the bustle of the half world that thrives in shade and starshine.

Leaning now on an elbow, he let his eyes rove among the beeches, into the bossy tops, solemn and sedate, and the deep recesses that might be full of the little folk of fairyland at their cantrips. And then farther back and above all was Dunchuach the stately, lifting its face, wood-bearded, to the stars!

"If a wind was here it was all I wanted," said Boboon, and when he said it the wind came – a salty air from the sea. The whole countryside cooled and gave out fresh scents of grass and earth.

"O God! O God!" cried the wanderer, "here we are out-by, the beasts and the birds and the best of Boboon together! Here is the place for ease and the full heart."

He up and ran into the town, and up to the captain's gate and in.

"Master," he cried, "it's the old story, – I must be taking the road for it; here's no rest for John Fine Macdonald!"

"But you'll leave the girl," said the captain, who saw the old fever in the man's eyes; "I have taken a notion of her, and – "

"So be it! let her bide."

"I'll marry her before the morn's out."

"Marry!" cried Boboon, putting back his hair from his face with a nervous hand. "You would marry a wanderer's child?"

"Well, they'll talk, no doubt; but she has gifts to make them forget, and she's good enough to make a king's woman."

"Sir," said Boboon, "I have but one thing to say, and that's our own Gaelic old-word, 'There are few lapdogs in a fox's litter.'"

The captain's face got as red as his vest, and he had a ready hand up for an answer to Boboon, but he had mind the man was the girl's father.

"I'll risk it," he said, "and you can go your wandering ways, for Betty is willing."

"No doubt, no doubt," said Boboon, and he went. In the hollow of the night he was hooting back like a boy at the hoolets on the slopes of Coillevraid, and at the mouth of day, in a silver wet light, he was standing on the edge of the hills that look on two lochs, his head high like a scenting deer's. He turned him round about to all airts with his eyes from Cruachan to Cowal, and as far between Knapdale and Lorn as a wanderer has vision, and yonder, down at Kames, was the camp of his clan!

Betty his daughter left Macvicar's Land in the morning and went to be captain's wife, with a seat in the kirk and callers from the castle itself.

"Wait, wait," said old Craignure, when the tale reached him, "you'll see the fox come out on her ere long."

But the fox was not there; it was skipping a day, as the fox will do sometimes when the day before has been good hunting. All went well with the woman till the worst that might have been the best happened, and she died with her first child. It was the year of the stunted oats, that brought poverty to Inneraora and black bread to the captain's board; but black bread and brochan would have been the blithest of meat for him if Betty was left to share it. He took to the bottle, and left the boy to women who had no skill of wild youth.

And the child grew like a fir-tree, straight and tall, full of hot blood, swung about by whim and the moment's fancy. For him it was ever the horse and gun, a snatched dinner and hearty, and off to the wood or hill. He got to know the inner ways of the beasts that hide in the coarse grasses and the whin; at a whistle he could coax flapping birds to come to heel. A loose vest and a naked neck for ever were marring his gentility, and his closest friends were countrymen with hard hands and the loud ready laugh.

One day it came to the captain's mind that something must be made of this young blade, and he sent for him.

"Boy," said he, "are you at your books?"

"No, but – but I ken a short way with the badgers," the lad made answer.

"Did you have a lesson this morning?"

"Never a lesson," said the lad; "I was too busy living."

"Living, said ye?"

"Living. I was at the swimming at the Creags, and beaking in the sun on the braes above the Garron beside the march wall where the hedgehogs creep, and I am new from the shinty," and he shook the shinty-stick in his hand.

The captain took to pondering, his chin on his hand and his elbows on the table, where a bottle and glass lay beside him.

After a bit he said, "Look ye, my son, what are ye meaning to be?"

"I'm for the sword-work," the lad said, in a flash, his face twitching.

"I would sooner see you in hell first!" cried the captain, thumping the board till the glass rang. He had seen foreign wars himself and had a hack on the groin.

That was the first of the feud between them.

They fought it dour and they fought it hard, the father for the crafts of peace and the lad for his own way, and at last one day the captain said –

"To the door, brat, and your lair with the Boboons you belong to! Faith, and your grandfather was right when he said there was never a lap-dog in a fox's litter."

Who he came of, the lad had no notion, for the swart Macdonalds never came near the town after Boboon left it for the last time; but he put on his bonnet, and went out of the house and on to the highroad.

It was well on to winter, a brawling day, with the leaves of the Duke's trees swishing thick and high over the thatch and through the streets of the Duke's town. Snug stood the gables, friendly and warm, and the window-lozens winked with the light of big peat-fires within. Over the breast the sea-birds yelped and crows craked without a stop, stirring about in the branches behind Macvicar's Land. And the salt wind! It blew in from the low bay at one end of the town and through it to the other, and before it went a lad into the wide world that starts at the factor's corner.

"By the shore-side to the low country, or by the woods to the hills?" the lad asked himself. He had the *caman* still in his hand, and he tossed it in the air. "*Bas* for the highway, *cas* for the low," said he. The shinty fell *bas*, and our hero took to it for the highway to the north. He swithered at the Arches, and looked back on the front of the town and the quay with the oil-lights on it. He was half in the humour to bide, but he put the notion behind him and stretched to the brae, whistling a piper's march. At the head of the brae the town houses were lost to him, and this so soon he could not put up with, so he went down on a way to the right a little and stood on the grass of the Winterton field.

Fast and dark the night was falling, a heavy smirr of rain was drooking the grass, and the trees on every hand shook the water in blobs from the branches. Through them the lights of the finest town in the world shone damp and woe-begone.

"There are good folk in't, and bad folk in't," said the lad to himself; "but somehow 'twas never the place for me!"

He turned and went into the road through the wood, savage at heart, without a thought of where his sleep would be. When he came to Kennachregan, there was the scad of a fire above the trees beside the roar-ing river, and he went down and looked over a march dyke at a band of wanderers under the trees. Young and old, men and women, they lay steaming on soft beds of springy spruce-branches with their toes to the crackling logs, snoring as snore sound sleepers, sheltered from the rain by the thick branches, the side of the hill, and here and there a canvas covering. There was but one of them up – a long old man with lank jaws and black eyes – John Fine Macdonald. He was stirring up the logs with the shod of a crutch and humming a Perth song, and before the hottest of the fire a plucked bird was roasting.

The smell of the meat and the wood-fire rose to the dykeside where the lad stood shivering in his wet clothes, and the comfort of the camp was something he could not pass by.

He took a jump over the dyke and went out in the light of the fire, wondering what would be his welcome. Old Boboon looked up with his hand over his eyes, then rose on his crutches and put a hand on the young fellow's shoulder.

"You're from Inneraora town?" said he.

"I am," said the lad; "but it's Inneraora no more for me."

"Ho! ho!" laughed the old wanderer. "Sit ye down, ye scamp, and take your fingers to a pick of your grandfather's hen. Boboon's children may be slow and far, but home's aye home to them!"

The Fell Sergeant

IT is ill enough to have to die in Glenaora at any season, but to get the word for travelling from it on yon trip in the spring of the year is hard indeed. The gug-gug will halloo in your ears to bid you bide a wee and see the red of the heather creep on Tom-an-dearc; the soft and sap-scented winds will come in at the open door, and you will mind, maybe, of a day long-off and lost when you pulled the copper leaves of the bursting oak and tossed them among a girl's hair. Oh! the long days and the strong days! They will come back to you like the curious bit in a tune that is vexatious and sweet, and not for words or a set thought. You will think of the lambs on the slopes, of the birds tearing through the thousand ways in the woods, of the magic hollows in below the thick-sown pines, of the burns, deep at the bottom of *eas* and corri, spilling like gold on a stair. And then, it may be, Solomon Carrier's cart goes by to the town, the first time since the drifts went off the high road; you hear the clatter of the iron shoes, and your mind will go with him to the throng street where the folks are so kind and so free.

But to turn your back for the last at that time on Lecknamban must come sorest of all. For Lecknamban has seven sheilings hidden in its hills, where the grass is long and juicy, and five burns that are aye on the giggle like girls at a wedding, and the Aora daunders down in front of the knowe, full of fish for the Duke alone, but bonny for earl or caird.

It was in this same glen, in this same Lecknamban, in the spring of a year, a woman was at her end. She was a woman up in years but not old, a black Bana-Mhuileach who had seen pleasant things and trials like all who come to this queer market-place; but now when the time was come to take the long road with no convoy, only the good times were in her recollection. And though Glenaora was not her calf-country (for she came but a year ago to bide with a friend), she was swear't to turn heel on a place so cosy.

She sat propped up in a box-bed, on pillows, with her face to the open door, and the friendly airs of the countryside came in to stir her hair. With them came scents of the red earth and the grass, birch-tree and myrtle, from the moor. But more than all they brought her who was at her end a keen craving for one more summer of the grand world. Strong in her make and dour at the giving-in, she kept talking of the world's affairs and fool-ishness to the folk about her who were waiting the Almighty's will and the coming of the stretching-board. Her fingers picked without a stop at the woolly bits of the blankets, and her eyes were on as much of the knowe below the house as she could see out at the open door. It was yellow at the foot with flowers, and here and there was a spot of blue from the cuckoo-brogue.

"Women, women," she said with short breaths, "I'm thinking aye, when I see the flowers, of a man that came from these parts to Duart. He sang 'Mo Nighean Dubh' in a style was never heard before in our place, and he once brought me the scented cuckoo-brogues from Aora."

Said the goodwife, "Aoirig, poor woman, it is not the hour for ancient old *sgeuls;* be thinking of a canny going."

"Going! it was aye going with me," said the woman in the bed. "And it was aye going when things were at their best and I was the keener for them."

"It's the way of God, my dear, *ochanie!*" said one of the two Tullich sisters, putting a little salt in a plate for the coming business.

"O God! it's the hard way, indeed. And I'm not so old as you by two or three clippings."

"Peace, Aoirig, heart; you had your own merry times, and that's as much as most of us have claim to"

"Merry times! merry times!" said Aoirig, humped among the bedding, her mind wandering.

Curls of the peat-reek coiled from the floor among the *cabars* or through the hole in the roof; a lamb ran by the door bleating for its mother, and the whistling of an *uiseag* high over the grass where his nest lay ran out to a thin thread of song. The sound of it troubled the dying woman, and she asked her friends to shut the door. Now and again Maisie would put a wet cloth to her lips and dry the death-sweat from her face. The goodwife was throng among chests and presses looking for sheets, shrouds, and dead-caps.

"It's a pity," said she, "you brought no grave-clothes with you from Mull, my dear."

"Are you grudging me yours?" asked Aoirig, coming round from wandering.

"No, nor grudging; fine ye ken it, cousin. But I know ye have them, and it's a pity you should be dressed in another's spinning than your own."

"Ay, they're yonder sure enough: clean and ready. And there's more than that beside them. The linen I should have brought to a man's home."

"You and your man's home! Is it Duart, my dear, among your own folk, or down to Inishail, you would have us take you?"

Aoirig coughed till the red froth was at her lips.

"Duart is homely and Inishail is holy, sure enough, but I would have it Kilmalieu. They tell me it's a fine kirkyard; but I never had the luck to see it."

"It's well enough, I'll not deny, and it would not be so far to take you.

Our folk have a space of their own among the MacVicars, below the parson."

The woman in the bed signed for a sip of water, and they had it fast at her lips.

"Could you be putting me near the Macnicols?" she asked in a weakening voice. "The one I speak of was a Macnicol."

"Ay, ay," said the goodwife; "they were aye gallant among the girls."

"Gallant he was," said the one among the blankets. "I see him now. The best man ever I saw. It was at a wedding – "

The woman's breast racked and the spume spattered over the homespun blankets.

Maisie was heating a death-shift at the peat-fire, turning it over in her hands, letting the dry airs into every seam and corner.

Looking at her preparation, the dying woman caught back her breath to ask why such trouble with a dead-shift.

"Ye would not have it on damp and cold," said Maisie, settling the business. "I doubt it'll be long in the sleeves, woman, for the goodwife has a lengthy reach."

"It was at a marriage in Glenurchy," said Aoirig in a haver, the pillows slipping down behind her back. "Yonder he is. A slim straight lad. Ronnal, O Ronnal my hero! What a dancer! not his match in Mull. Aye so – "

A foot could be heard on the road, and one of the two sisters ran out, for she knew whom it would be. They had sent word to the town by Solomon in the morning for Macnicol the wright to come up with the stretching-board, thinking there was but an hour more for poor Aoirig.

Macnicol's were the footsteps, and there he was with the stretching-board under his arm – a good piece of larch rubbed smooth by sheet and shroud, and a little hollow worn at the head. He was a fat man, rolling a bit to one side on a short leg, gross and flabby at the jowl, and thick-lipped; but he might have been a swanky lad in his day, and there was a bit of good-humour in the corner of his eye, where you will never see it when one has been born with the uneasy mind. He was humming to himself as he came up the brae a Badenoch ditty they have in these parts on the winter nights, gossiping round the fire. Whom he was going to stretch he had no notion, except that it was a woman and a stranger to the glen.

The sister took him round to the corner of the house and in at the byre door, and told him to wait. "It'll not be long now," she said.

"Then she's still to the fore," said the wright. "I might have waited on the paymaster's dram at Three Bridges if I had ken't. Women are aye thrawn about dying. They'll put it off to the last, when a man would be glad to be taking the road. Who is she, poor woman?"

"A cousin-german of Nanny's," said the sister, putting a bottle before him, and whipping out for some bannock and cheese. He sat down on a shearing-stool, facing the door, half open, between the byre he was in and the kitchen where Aoirig was at the dying. The stretching-board leaned against the wall outside.

"Aye so gentle, so kind," the woman in the bed was saying in her last dover. "He kissed me first on a day like this. And the blue flowers from Aora?"

In the byre the wright was preeing the drink and paying little heed to food. It was the good warm stuff they brew on the side of Lochow, the heart of the very heart of the barley-fields, with the taste of gall and peat, and he mellowed with every quaich, and took to the soft lilting of Niall Ban's song:

> "'I am the Sergeant fell but kind
> (Ho! ho! heroes, *agus ho-e-ro!*);
> I only lift but the deaf and blind,
> The wearied-out and the rest-inclined.
> Many a booty I drive before,
> Through the glens, through the glens,' said the Sergeant Mor."

Ben the house the goodwife was saying the prayers for the dying woman the woman should have said for herself while she had the wind for it, but Aoirig harped on her love-tale. She was going fast, and the sisters, putting their hands to her feet, could feel that they were cold as the rocks. Maisie's arms were round her, and she seemed to have the notion that here was the grip of death, for she pushed her back.

"I am not so old – so old. There is Seana, my neighbour at Duart – long past the four-score and still spinning – I am not so old – God of grace – so old – and the flowers – "

A grey shiver went over her face; her breast heaved and fell in; her voice stopped with a gluck in the throat.

The women stirred round fast in the kitchen. Out on the clay floor the two sisters pushed the table and laid a sheet on it, the goodwife put aside the pillows and let Aoirig's head fall back on the bed. Maisie put her hand to the clock and stopped it.

"Open the door, open the door!" cried the goodwife, turning round in a hurry and seeing the door still shut.

One of the sisters put a finger below the sneck and did as she was told, to let out the dead one's ghost.

Outside, taking the air, to get the stir of the strong waters out of his head, was the wright.

He knew what the opening of the door meant, and he lifted his board and went in with it under his arm. A wafting of the spring smells came in at his back, and he stood with his bonnet in his hand.

"So this is the end o't?" he said in a soft way, stamping out the fire on the floor.

He had but said it when Aoirig sat up with a start in the bed, and the women cried out. She opened her eyes and looked at the man, with his fat face, his round back, and ill-made clothes, and the death-deal under his oxter, and then she fell back on the bed with her face stiffening.

"Here's the board for ye," said the wright, his face spotted white and his eyes staring. "I'll go out a bit and take a look about me. I once knew a woman who was terribly like yon, and she came from Mull."

Black Murdo

"Mas breug uam e is breug thugam e."
— GAELIC PROVERB

I

BLACK MURDO's wife was heavy, and 'twas the time the little brown nuts were pattering in Stronbuie wood. Stronbuie spreads out its greenness to the sun from the slope of Cladich. It is, in its season, full of the piping of birds and the hurry of wings, and the winds of it have the smell of a fat soil. The Diarmaids were the cunning folk to steal it; for if Stronshira is good, Stronbuie is better; and though the loops of Aora tangle themselves in the gardens of the Red Duke, Lochow has enchantment for the galley of a king. Fraoch Eilean, Innis Chonell, and Innis Chonain – they cluster on the bend of it like the gems on a brooch, Inishail of the Monks makes it holy, and Cruachan-ben, who lords it over Lorn, keeps the cold north wind from the shore. They may talk of Glenaora, but Stronbuie comes close, close to the heart!

For all that, 'twas on a time a poor enough place for a woman in yon plight; for the rest of the clan crowded down on Innistrynich, all fighters and coarse men of the sword, and a skilly woman or a stretching-board was no nearer than a day's tramp over the hill and down Aora glen to the walls of Inneraora. If one died on Cladich-side then – and 'twas a dying time, for the Athol dogs were for ever at the harrying – it was but a rough burying, with no corranach and no mort-cloth; if a child came, it found but cold water and a cold world, whatever hearts might be. But for seven years no child came for Black Murdo.

They say, in the Gaelic old-word, that a stolen bitch will never throw clean pups nor a home-sick woman giants. Murdo recked nothing of that when he went wooing in a time of truce to Croit-bhile, the honey-croft that makes a red patch on the edge of Creag Dubh. He brought Silis home to the dull place at Stronbuie, and she baked his bannocks and ploughed his bit of soil, but her heart never left salt Finne-side. In the morning she would go to the hill to look through the blurred glen, and she would have made bargains with the ugliest crow that could flap on feathers for a day's use of his wings. She could have walked it right often and gaily to her people's place, but Black Murdo was of Clan Artair, and Artairich had not yet come under the *bratach* of Diarmaid, and bloody knives made a march-dyke between the two tartans.

Seven years and seven days went by, and Black Murdo, coming in on an evening after a hard day at the deer, found Silis making the curious wee clothes. He looked at her keen, questioning, and she bleached to the lips.

"So!" said he.

"Just so," said she, breaking a thread with her teeth, and bending till the peat-flame dyed her neck like wine.

"God, and I'm the stout fellow!" said he, and out he went, down all the way to Portinsherrich, and lusty he was with the ale among the pretty men there.

Weeks chased each other like sheep in a fank, and Silis grew sick at the heart. There's a time for a woman when the word of a woman is sweeter than a harp; but there were only foolish girls at Innistrynich, and coarse men of the sword. So Murdo stayed in from the roes when the time crept close. To see him do the heavy work of the house and carrying in the peats was a sorry sight.

Silis kept dreaming of Finne-side, where she had heard the long wave in the spring of the year when she had gone home on a pass-word to a woman's wedding with Long Coll. The same Long Coll had brothers, and one had put a man's foolish sayings in her ears before ever she met Murdo, she a thin girl like a saugh-wand and not eighteen till Beltane. They called him – no matter – and he had the way with the women. Faith, it's the strange art! It is not looks, nor dancing, nor the good heart, nor wit, but some soft fire of the eye and maybe a song to the bargain. Whatever it was, it had Silis, for all that her good man Murdo had a man's qualities and honesty extra.

They say, *"Cnuic is sluic is Alpeinich, ach cuin a thàinig Artharaich?"* [1] in the by-word; but Artharaich had age enough for a *taibhsear* whatever, for Black Murdo had the Sight.

It's the curious thing to say of a man with all his parts that he should be *taibhsear* and see visions; for a *taibhsear*, by all the laws, should be an old fellow with little use for swords or shinny-sticks. But Murdo missed being a full *taibhsear* by an ell, so the fit had him seldom. He was the seventh son of a mother who died with the brand of a cross on her brow, and she was kin to the Glenurchy Woman. And something crept over him with the days, that put a mist in his eyes when he looked at Silis; but "I'm no real *taibhsear*," he said to himself, "and I swear by the black stones it is no cloth. A man with all the Gift might call it a shroud high on her breast, but – "

"Silis, *a bhean!* shall it be the Skilly Dame of Inneraora?"

A light leaped to the woman's eyes, for the very thing was in her mind.

---

[1] *The hills and hollows and Clan Alpine came together, but when arose Clan Artair?*

"If it could be," she said, slowly; "but it's not easy to get her, for black's your name on Aoraside."

"Black or white, Murdo stands in his own shoes. He has been at the gate of Inneraora when Strong Colin the warder had little thought of it."

"Then, oh heart! it must be soon – to-morrow – but – "

The mouth of day found Silis worse, and Murdo on his way to Inneraora.

He stepped it down Glenaora like Coll Mor in the story, or the man with the fairy shoes. A cloud was over Tullich and a wet wind whistled on Kennachregan. The man's target played dunt on his back, so hasty was he, for all that the outposts of Big Colin had hawk's eyes on the pass. He had got the length of Alt Shelechan when a Diarmaid came out on him from the bracken with a curse on his mouth. He was a big Diarmaid, high-breasted and stark, for there's no denying there was breed in the pigs.

"Ho, ho, lad!" said he, crously, "it's risking it you are this day!"

Black Murdo's hands went to his sides, where a ready man's should ready be; but he had sight of Silis. He could see her in Stronbuie in the bothy, on the wee creepy-stool beside the peats, and he knew she was saying the Wise Woman's Wish that Diarmaid mothers have so often need of. Length is length, and it's a far cry to Lochow sure enough; but even half a *taibhsear* takes no count of miles and time.

He spoke softly. "I go to Inneraora for the Skilly Woman. My wife is a daughter of your folks, and she'll have none but the dame who brought herself home."

"Death or life?" asked the Diarmaid, a freckled hand still on the basket-hilt. He put the question roughly, for nobody likes to lose a ploy.

"Life it is, my lad. It's not to dress corpses but to wash weans she's wanted."

"Ho-chutt!" went the blade back against the brass of the scabbard (for he was *duin'-uasal* who carried it), and the man's face changed.

"Pass!" he said. "I would not stand in a bairn's way to life. Had it been shrouds instead of sweelers, we could have had it out, for a corpse is in no great hurry. But troth it's yourself is the tight one, and I would have liked a bit of the old game."

"No more than Murdo, red fellow!"

"Murdo! So be't; yet Murdo will give me his dirk for gate-pay, or they'll be saying farther down that Calum, as good a man, kept out of his way."

The *biodag* went flying into the grass at Calum's feet, and Murdo went leaping down the glen. It was like stalking deer for the Diarmaids. Here and there he had to go into the river or among the hazel-switches, or crawl on his stomach among the gall. From Kilmune to Uchdanbarracaldine the red fellows were passing, or playing with the *clachneart* or the *cabar*, or watching their women toiling in the little fields.

"Thorns in their sides!" he said to himself, furious at last, when another keen-eyed Diarmaid caught sight of his tartan and his black beard among some whins. It was a stripling with only a dirk, but he could gather fifty men on the crook of his finger.

"Stand!" cried the Diarmaid, flashing the dirk out. "What want ye so far over this way?"

Murdo, even in the rage, saw Silis, a limp creature sweating in her pains, her black eyes (like the sloe) keen on the door. So close, so sure, so sorrowful! He could have touched her on the shoulder and whispered in her ear.

"I am Black Murdo," he told the lad. "I am for Inneraora for the Skilly Woman for my wife, child of your own clan."

"Death or life?"

"Life."

"'Tis a bonny targe ye have, man; it might be doing for toll."

The lad got it, and Murdo went on his way. He found the Skilly Woman, who put before him sourmilk and brose. But he would not have drink or sup, so back through the Diarmaids they went without question (for the woman's trade was as good as the chief's convoy), till they came to Tom-an-dearc. Out upon them there a fellow red and pretty.

"Hold!" he said, as if it had been dogs. "What's the name of ye, black fellow?"

Murdo cursed in his beard. "My name's honest man, but I have not time to prove it."

"Troth that's a pity. But seeing there's the *cailleach* with you, you must e'en go your way. There's aye some of you folk on the stretching-board. Ye want heart, and ye die with a flaff of wind. Lend me your sword, *'ille!*"

"Squint-mouth!" cried Murdo, "your greedy clan took too much off me this day already for me to part with the sweetest blade Gow-an-aora ever beat on iron. I took it from one of your cowards at Carnus, and if it's back it goes, it's not with my will."

"Then it's the better man must have it," said the red fellow, and, Lord, he was the neat-built one!

They took off their coats, and for lack of bucklers rolled them round their arms, both calm and canny. The Diarmaid was first ready with his brand out, and Murdo put to his point. For a little the two men stood, spread out, hard-drawn behind the knees, with the cords of the neck like thongs, then at it with a clatter of steel.

The Skilly Woman, with the plaid pulled tight over her grey hair, sat with sunk eyes on a stone and waited without wonder. She had sons who had died in brawls at Kilmichael market, or in the long foray far in Kintail; and her man, foster-brother to a chief, got death in the strange foreign wars, where the pay was not hide and horn but round gold.

A smoky soft smirr of rain filled all the gap between the hills, though Sithean Sluaidhe and Dunchuach had tips of brass from a sun dropping behind the Salachary hills. The grass and the gall lost their glitter and became grey and dull; the hill of Lecknamban, where five burns are born, coaxed the mist down on its breast like a lover. It was wet, wet, but never a drop made a rush bend or a leaf fall. Below the foot the ground was greasy, as it is in a fold at the dipping-time; but the two men pulled themselves up with a leap on it as if it might be dry sand, and the brogues made no error on the soil.

First the Diarmaid pressed, for he had it over the other man in youth, and youth is but tame when it's slow or slack. Murdo waited, all eyes that never blinked, with the basket well up, and kept on his toes. "Splank, sp-ll-ank, sp-ll-ank – *siod e!*" said the blades, and the Diarmaid's for a time made the most of the music, but he never got inside the black fellow's guard. Then Murdo took up the story with a snap of the teeth, skelping hard at the red one till the hands dirled in the basket like a bag of pins. The smirr gathered thicker, and went to rain that fell solid, the brogues grew like steeped bladders on the feet, a scatter of crows made a noisy homing to the trees at Tullich, and Aora gobbled like swine in a baron's trough.

"Haste ye, heroes," said the old woman, cowering on the wet stone; "haste ye, dears; it's mighty long ye are about it."

The Diarmaid turned the edge twice on the coated arm, and Murdo wasted his wind to curse. Then he gave the stroke that's worth fifty head of kyloes (fine they know that same all below Cladich!), and a red seam jumped to the Diarmaid's face. All his heart went to stiffen his slacking heavy arm, and he poured on Murdo till Murdo felt it like a rain of spears. One hot wandering stroke he got on the bonnet, and for want of the bowl of brose at Inneraora, the wind that should go to help him went inside, and turned his stomach. Sweat, hot and salt, stung his eyes, his ears filled with a great booming, he fell in a weary dream of a far-off fight on a witched shore, with the waves rolling, and some one else at the fencing, and caring nought, but holding guard with the best blade Gow-an-aora ever took from flame. Back stepped the Diarmaid, sudden, and sweep went his steel at the shaking knees.

A bairn's cry struck Murdo's ear through the booming and sent him full awake. He drew back the stretched foot fast, and round the red one's sword hissed through air. "Foil! foil!" said Murdo, and he slashed him on the groin.

"That'll do, man; no more," said the Skilly Woman, quickly.

"I may as well finish him; it's lame he'll be all his days any way, and little use is a man with a halt in a healthy clan."

"Halt or no halt, let him be; he's my second cousin's son."

Murdo looked for a bit at the bloody thing before him, but the woman craved again with bony fingers on his wrist; so he spat on the dirty green tartan and went. The smoke rose from him and hung about with a smell of wearied flesh, the grey of the mist was black at Carnus. When the pair came over against Lochow, where one can see the holy isle when it is day, the night was deep and cold; but the woman bent at the cross with a "*Mhoire Mhathair,*" and so did the man, picking the clotted blood from his ear. They dropped down the brae on the house at last.

For a little Black Murdo's finger hung on the sneck, and when he heard a sound he pushed in the door.

All about the house the peat-reek swung like mist on the mountain. Wind and rain fought it out on Cladich brae, and when it was not the wind that came bold through the smoke-hole in the roof, 'twas the rain, a beady slant that hissed on the peats like roasting herrings. The woman lay slack on the bed, her eyes glossed over with the glass that folks see the great sights through, and her fingers making love over the face and breast of a new-born boy that cried thinly at her knees. A lighted cruisie spluttered with heavy smell at the end of a string on a rafter.

"O Skilly Woman, Skilly Woman, it's late we are," said Black Murdo.

"Late enough, as ye say, just man. Had ye bartered an old sword for twenty minutes on the Tom-an-dearc, I was here before danger."

Then the Skilly Woman set him on the wet windy side of the door, and went about with busy hands.

The man, with the ragged edge of his kilt scraping his knees and the rain bubbling in his brogues, leaned against the wattled door and smeared the blood from his brow. A cold wind gulped down from Glenurchy and ghosts were over Inishail. The blast whirled about and whirled about, and swung the rowan like a fern, and whistled in the gall, and tore the thatch, all to drown a child's cry. The blackness crowded close round like a wall, and flapped above like a plaid – Stronbuie was in a tent and out of the world. Murdo strained to hear a voice, but the wind had the better of him. He went round to the gable, thinking to listen at the window, but the board on the inside shut the wind and him out. The strange emptiness of grief was in his belly.

Inside, the Skilly One went like a witch, beak-nosed and half-blind. There was clatter of pans and the dash of water, the greeting of the child and the moan of the mother. What else is no man's business. For all she was skilly the old dame had no thought of the woman sinking.

"You'll have blithe-meat in the morning," she said, cheerily, from the fireside.

Silis made worse moan than before.

"Such a boy, white love! And hair like the copper! His hide is mottled like a trout's back; calf of my heart!"

Silis, on her side, put out white craving arms. "Give it to me, wife; give it to me."

"Wheesht! rest ye, dear, rest ye," said the Skilly Dame.

But she put the bairn in its mother's arms. Silis, when she had it on her breast, sobbed till the bed shook.

"Is not he the hero, darling?" said the Skilly Woman. "It's easy seen he's off Clan Diarmaid on one side, for all that your hair is black as the sloe. Look at the colour of him!"

Fright was in the mother's face. "Come close, come close till I tell you," she said, her long hair damp on her milky shoulders.

The Skilly Woman put down her head and listened with wonder.

"Me-the-day! Was I not the blind one to miss it? His name, white love? No one shall ken it from me, not even Murdo."

A man's name took up the last breath of Silis; she gave a little shiver, and choked with a sound that the old crone had heard too often not to know.

She looked, helpless, for a little at the bed, then felt the mother's feet. They were as cold as stone.

A cry caught Murdo's ear against the wattles, and he drove in the door with his shoulder, heeding no sneck nor bar.

"Am not I the blind fool?" said the crone. "There's your wife gone, cheap enough at the price of a yard of steel."

They stood and looked at the bed together, the bairn crying without notice.

"I knew it," said the man, heaving; "*taibhsear* half or whole, I could see the shroud on her neck!"

The grey light was drifting in from Cladich. The fir-trees put stretched fingers up against the day, and Murdo was placing a platter of salt on a bosom as cold and as white as the snow.

"You're feeding him on the wrong cloth," said he, seeing the crone give suck to the child from a rag of Diarmaid tartan dipped in goat's milk.

II

THE boy grew like a tree in a dream, that is seed, sapling, and giant in one turn on the side. Stronbuie's wattled bothy, old and ugly, quivered with his laughing, and the young heather crept closer round the door. The Spotted Death filled Inishail with the well-fed and the warm-happed; but the little one, wild on the brae, forgotten, sucking the whey from rags and robbing the bush of its berries, gathered sap and sinew like the child of kings. It is the shrewd way of God! There was bloody enough work forby, for never a sheiling passed but the brosey folks came pouring down Glenstrae, scythe, sword, and spear, and went back with the cattle before them, and redness and smoke behind. But no raider put hand on Black Murdo, for now he was *taibhsear* indeed, and the *taibhsear* has magic against club or steel. How he became *taibhsear* who can be telling? When he buried Silis out on the isle, his heart grew heavy, gloom seized him, the cut of the Diarmaid's sword gave a quirk to his brain that spoiled him for the world's use. He took to the hills no more in sport, he carried Gow-an-aora's sword no more in battle, for all that it cost him so dear. A poor man's rig was his at the harvest because of his Gift, and the cailzie cock or the salmon never refused his lure.

Skill of the claymore, the seven cuts, and yon ready slash worth fifty head of kyloes, he gave to the boy, and then the quick cunning parry, and the use of the foot and knee that makes half a swordsman.

But never a spot of crimson would he have on Rory's steel.

"First dip in the blood of the man with the halt, and then farewell to ye!" he said, wearying for the day when the boy should avenge his mother.

Folks – far-wandered ones – brought him news of the man with the halt that was his giving, the Diarmaid whose bargain for a sword on Tom-an-dearc cost Silis her life. He passed it on to the boy, and he filled him with old men's tales. He weaved the cunning stories of the pigs of Inneraora, for all that the boy's mother came from their loins, and he made them – what there may well be doubts of – cowards and weak.

"They killed your mother, Rory: her with the eyes like the sloe and the neck like snow. Swear by the Holy Iron that the man with the halt we ken of gets his pay for it."

Rory swore on the iron. It is an easy thing for one when the blood is strong and the *biodag* still untried. He lay awake at night, thinking of his mother's murderer till the sweat poured. He would have been on the track of him before ever he had won his man's bonnet by lifting the *clach-cuid-fear,* but Murdo said, "Let us be sure. You are young yet, and I have one other trick of fencing worth while biding for."

At last, upon a time, Murdo found the boy could match himself, and he said, "Now let us to this affair."

He took the boy, as it were, by the hand, and they ran up the hills and down the hills, and through the wet glens, to wherever a Diarmaid might be; and where were they not where strokes were going? The hoodie-crow was no surer on the scent of war. Blar-na-leine took them over the six valleys and the six mountains; Cowal saw them on the day the Lamonts got their bellyful; a knock came on them on the night when the Stewarts took their best from Appin and flung themselves on Inneraora, and they went out without a word and marched with that high race.

But luck was with the man with the halt they sought for. At muster for raid, or at market, he was there, swank man and pretty but for the lameness he had found on an ill day on Tom-an-dearc. He sang songs round the ale with the sweetness of the bird, and his stories came ready enough off the tongue. Black Murdo and the boy were often close enough on his heel, but he was off and away like the corp-candle before they were any nigher. If he had magic, it could have happened no stranger.

Once, a caird who went round the world with the jingle of cans on his back and a sheaf of withies in his oxter, told them that a lame Diarmaid was bragging at Kilmichael fair that he would play single-stick for three days against the countryside. They sped down to Ford, and over the way; but nothing came of it, for the second day had found no one to come to the challenge, and the man with the halt was home again.

Black Murdo grew sick of the chase, and the cub too tired of it. For his father's fancy he was losing the good times – many a fine exploit among the Atholmen and the brosey folks of Glenstrae; and when he went down to Innistrynich to see the lads go out with belt and plaid, he would give gold to be with them.

One day, "I have dreamed a dream," said Murdo. "Our time is come: what we want will be on the edge of the sea, and it will be the third man after dawn. Come, son, let us make for Inneraora."

Inneraora lies now between the bays, sleeping day and night, for the old times are forgot and the nettle's on Dunchuach. Before the plaid of MacCailein Mor was spread from Cowal to Cruachan, it was the stirring place; high and dry on the bank of Slochd-a-chubair, and the dogs themselves fed on buck-flesh from the mountains, so rowth the times! One we ken of has a right to this place or that place yonder that shall not be named, and should hold his head as high on Aora as any chief of the boar's snout; but *mo thruaigh! mo thruaigh!* the black bed of Macartair is in the Castle itself, and Macartair is without soil or shield. How Diarmaid got the old place is a sennachie's tale. "As much of the land as a heifer's hide will cover," said the foolish writing, and MacCailein had the guile to make the place his own. He cut the hide of a long-backed heifer into thin thongs, and stretched it round Stronbuie. There is day about to be seen with his race for that!

Over to Inneraora then went Murdo, and Rory clad for fighting, bearing with him the keen old sword. 'Twas a different time going down the glen then from what it was on the misty day Murdo fetched the Skilly Dame; for the Diarmaids he met by the way said, "'Tis the Lochow *taibhsear* and his tail," and let them by without a word, or maybe with a salute. They went to the Skilly Dame's house, and she gave them the Gael's welcome, with bannocks and crowdie, *marag-dhubh* and ale. But she asked them not their business, for that is the way of the churl. She made them soft-scented beds of white hay in a dirty black corner, where they slept till cock-crow with sweet weariness in their bones.

The morning was a grey day with frost and snow. Jumping John's bay below the house was asleep with a soft smoke like a blanket over it. Lean deer from behind the wood came down trotting along the shore, sniffing the saltness, and wondering where the meat was. With luck and a good *sgian-dubh* a quick lad could do some gralloching. The tide was far out from Ard Rannoch to the Gallowstree, and first there was the brown wrack, and then there was the dun sand, and on the edge of the sand a bird went stalking. The old man and the young one stood at the gable and looked at it all.

It was a short cut from below the castle to the point of Ard Rannoch, if the tide was out, to go over the sand. "What we wait on," said Murdo, softly, "goes across there. There will be two men, and them ye shall not heed, but the third is him ye ken of. Ye'll trap him between the whin-bush and the sea, and there can be no escaping unless he takes to the swimming for it."

Rory plucked his belts tight, took out the good blade wondrous quiet, breathing fast and heavy. The rich blood raced up his back, and tingled hot against his ruddy neck.

"What seest thou, my son?" said Murdo at last.

"A man with a quick step and no limp," quoth the lad.

"Let him pass."

Then again said the old man, "What seest thou?"

"A *bodach* frail and bent, with a net on his shoulder," said Rory.

"Let him pass."

The sun went high over Ben Ime, and struck the snow till the eyes were blinded. Rory rubbed the sweat from his drenched palm on the pleat of his kilt, and caught the basket-hand tighter. Over Aora mouth reek went up from a fishing-skiff, and a black spot stood out against the snow.

"What seest thou now, lad?" asked Murdo.

"The man with the halt," answered the lad.

"Then your time has come, child. The stroke worth the fifty head, and pith on your arm!"

Rory left the old man's side, and went down through a patch of shelisters, his mouth dry as a peat and his heart leaping. He was across the wrack and below the pools before the coming man had noticed him. But the coming man thought nothing wrong, and if he did, it was but one man at any rate, and one man could use but one sword, if swords were going. Rory stepped on the edge of the sand, and tugged the bonnet down on his brow, while the man limped on between him and the sea. Then he stepped out briskly and said, "Stop, pig!" He said it strangely soft, and with, as it were, no heart in the business; for though the lame man was strong, deep-breasted, supple, and all sound above the belt, there was a look about him that made the young fellow have little keenness for the work.

"Pig?" said the Diarmaid, putting back his shoulders and looking under his heavy brows. "You are the Lochow lad who has been seeking for me?"

"Ho, ho! red fellow; ye kent of it, then?"

"Red fellow! It's red enough you are yourself, I'm thinking. I have no great heed to draw steel on a lad of your colour, so I'll just go my way." And the man looked with queer wistful eyes over his shoulder at the lad, who, with blade-point on the sand, would have let him pass.

But up-by at the house the *taibhsear* watched the meeting. The quiet turn it took was beyond his reading, for he had thought it would be but the rush, and the fast fall-to, and no waste of time, for the tide was coming in.

"White love, give him it!" he cried out, making for the shore. "He looks lame, but the pig's worth a man's first fencing."

Up went the boy's steel against the grey cloud, and he was at the throat of the Diarmaid like a beast. "Malison on your black heart, murderer!" he roared, still gripping his broadsword. The Diarmaid flung him off like a child, and put up his guard against the whisking of his blade.

"Oh, foolish boy!" he panted wofully as the lad pressed, and the grey light spread over sea and over shore. The quiet tide crawled in about their feet; birds wheeled on white feathers with mocking screams; the old man leaned on his staff and cheered the boy. The Diarmaid had all the coolness and more of art, and he could have ended the play as he wanted. But he only fended, and at last the slash worth fifty head found his neck. He fell on his side, with a queer twisted laugh on his face, saying "Little hero, ye fence – ye fence – "

"Haste ye, son! finish the thing!" said the *taibhsear,* all shaking, and the lad did as he was told, bocking at the spurt the blood made. He was pushing his dirk in the sand to clean it, when his eye fell on the Skilly Woman hirpling nimbly down to the shore. She was making a loud cry.

"God! God! it's the great pity about this," said she, looking at Murdo cutting the silver buttons off the corpse's jacket. "Ken ye the man that's there dripping?"

"The man's no more," said Rory, cool enough. "He has gone travelling, and we forgot to ask his name."

"Then if happy you would be, go home to Lochow, and ask it not, nor aught about him, if you wouldn't rue long. You sucked your first from a Diarmaid rag, and it was not for nothing."

Murdo drew back with a clumsy start from the dead man's side and looked down on his face, then at the boy's, queerly. "I am for off," said he at last with a sudden hurry. "You can follow if you like, red young one." And he tossed the dead man's buttons in Rory's face!

The Sea-Fairy of French Foreland

ONCE I saw a fairy King, and it was in the Castle up-by. The Castle took fire, and a fine blaze it made at the foot of Dunchuach. A boy, I ran with the rest to carry out the MacCailein's rich gear, and behold! I wandered and lost my way in that large place where is a window for every day in the year. Up the long stairs and through the far passages, and over the shining sounding floors went I, barefoot, with a feared eye on every hole and corner. At every door it was, "Surely now I'm with the folks at the fire"; but every door was a way into a quieter quietness, and the Castle was my own. I sat at last on a black chair that had a curious twisted back, and the tears went raining on the lap of my kilt.

Long, long I sat, and sore I grat, my mind full, not so much of my way lost, but of the bigness of things, and the notion of what it would be to have to live in a castle at night, with doors on every hand for ghosts to rap at, and crooked passages without end for gowsty winds to moan in. Thinks I, "The smallest hut in the town for me, with all plain before me, with the one door shut and my face to it, and the candlelight seeking into every crack and cranny!"

It was then that the fairy King came on me out of the sewed cloth hanging on the wall.

He was a dainty wee man, in our own tartan, with a steel plate on his breast baronly-style, and strange long curly hair. I ran my wet eyes down seven silver buttons the shape of salmon on the front of his vest before I let myself go, but go I must, so I put fast heels on my fright. I galloped with a frozen tongue through miles of the Duke's castle till a door brought me out on the grass of Cairnban, in front of the friendly bleeze that my own folks were pouring the stoups of water on.

That was the only time the quiet folk and I came to a meeting, though our family was always gleg at seeing things. A cousin-german once saw the fairy bull that puts up in Loch Steallaire-bhan behind the town. It came on a jaunt to the glen in the guise of a rich maiden, and my cousin, the son of the house, made love to her. One night – in a way that I need not mention – he found himself in her room combing down her yellow hair, and what was among her hair but fine sand that told the whole story? "You are a *gruagach* of the lake!" cried the lad, letting the comb drop on the floor, with his face white, and the thing turned to its own shape and went bellowing to the shore.

And there was a man – blessings with him! for he's here no more – who would always be going up on Sithean Sluaidhe to have troke with the wee people on that fine knowe. He would bring them tastings of honey and butter to put them in a good key, and there they would dance by the hour for his diversion to the piping of a piper who played on drones of grass with reeds made of the midge's thrapple.

Still, in all my time I know but one body who could find the way to the den of the Sea-Fairies, and she was a lass whose folks were in Ceannmor at the time the French traffickers were coming here to swap casks of claret wine for the finest herrings in the wide world.

It was her custom to go down on the hot days to the shore at the Waterfoot when the tide was far out, and the sand was crusting with salt in the sun, and the wrack-balls burst with the heat, and the water lay flat like oil, and lazy, for want of a breath of wind. Sometimes it would be the French Foreland she would seek, and sometimes Dalchenna; but when the Frenchmen were at the Foreland she kept clear of it by the counsel of a cautious father.

Up the loch they would sail, the Frenchmen, in their gabberts, and hove-to with their casks to change for the cured herrings. A curious people they were, not much like our own good Gaels in many a way, but black-avised and slim; still with some of the Gael's notions about them too, such as the humour of fighting and drinking and scouring the countryside for girls.

But it happened that one year they left behind them only a wine of six-waters, and did some other dirty tricks forbye, and there was for long a feud, so that the Frenchmen be-hooved to keep to their boats and bargain with the curers over the gun'le.

On a day at that time, Marseli that I speak of had been bathing at the Ceannmor rocks – having a crave for salt water the Ceannmor folks nowadays are not very namely for. When she had her gown on again, she went round to Dalchenna sands and out far to the edge of the tide, where she sat on a stone and took to the redding of her hair, that rolled in copper waves before the comb – rich, thick, and splendid.

Before her, the tide was on the turn so slow and soft that the edge of it lifted the dry sand like meal. All about on the weedy stones the tailor-tartans leaped like grasshoppers, the spout-fish stuck far out of the sand and took a fresh gloss on their shells from the sun.

You might seek from shire to shire for a handsomer maid. She was at the age that's a father's heartbreak, rounding out at the bosom and mellowing at the eyes; her skin was like milk, and the sigh was at her lips as

often as the song. But though she sighed, it was not for the Ceannmor fishermen, coarse-bearded, and rough in their courting; for she had vanity,
from her mother's side, and queer notions. The mother's family had been
rich in their day, with bards and thoughtful people among them.

"If a sea-fairy could see me now," said Marseli, "it might put him in the
notion to come this way again," and she started to sing the child-song –

> "Little folk, little folk, come to me,
> From the lobbies that lie below the sea."

So agad e! cried a gull at her back, so plainly that she turned fast to look,
and there was the fairy before her!

Up got Marseli, all shaking and ready to fly, but the fairy-man looked
harmless enough as he bowed low to her, and she stayed to put her hair
behind her ears and draw her gown closer.

He was a little delicate man the smallest of Marseli's brothers could
have put in his oxter, with close curled hair, and eyes as black as Ridir
Lochiel's waistcoat. His clothes were the finest of the fine, knee-breeches
with silk hose, buckled brogues, a laced jacket, and a dagger at his belt –
no more like a fairy of the knowe than the green tree's like the gall.

"You're quick enough to take a girl at her word," said Marseli, cunning
one, thinking to hide from him the times and times she had cried over the
sands for the little sea-folks to come in with the tide.

The fairy-man said something in his own tongue that had no sense for
the girl, and he bowed low again, with his bonnet waving in his hand, in
the style of Charlie Munn the dancer.

"You must speak in the Gaelic," said Marseli, still a bit put about; "or
if you have not the Gaelic, I might be doing with the English, though little
I care for it."

"Faith," said the fairy-man, "I have not the Gaelic, more's the pity, but
I know enough English to say you're the prettiest girl ever I set eyes on
since I left my own place."

(Ho! ho! was he not the cunning one? The fairies for me for gallantry!)

"One of such judgment can hardly be uncanny," thought Marseli, so
she stayed and cracked with him in the English tongue.

The two of them walked up over the sand to the birch-trees, and under
the birches the little fellow asked Marseli to sit down.

"You are bigger than I looked for in a sea-fairy," said she when the
crack was a little bit on.

"A fairy?" said the little fellow, looking at her in the flash of an eye.

"Yes! Though I said just now that you took one fast at her word, the
truth to tell is, that always when the tide went out I sang at your back-
doors the song you heard to-day for the first time. I learned it from Beann
Francie in the Horse Park."

The stranger had a merry laugh – not the roar of a Finne fisherman – and a curious way of hitching the shoulders, and the laugh and the shoulder-hitch were his answer for Marseli.

"You'll be a king in the sea – in your own place – or a prince maybe," said the girl, twisting rushes in her hand.

The man gave a little start and got red at the face.

"Who in God's name said so?" asked he, looking over her shoulder deep into the little birch-wood, and then uneasy round about him.

"I guessed it," said Marseli. "The kings of the land-fairies are by-ordinar big, and the dagger is ever on their hips."

"Well, indeed," said the little fellow, "to say I was king were a bravado, but I would not be just denying that I might be Prince."

And that way their friendship began.

At the mouth of many nights when the fishing-boats were off at the fishing, or sometimes even by day when her father and her two brothers were chasing the signs of sea-pig and scart far down on Tarbert, Marseli would meet her fairy friend in a cunning place at the Black-water foot, where the sea puts its arms well around a dainty waist of lost land. Here one can see Loch Finne from Ardno to Strathlachlan: in front lift the long lazy Cowal hills, and behind is Auchnabreac wood full of deer and birds. Nowadays the Duke has his road round about this cunning fine place, but then it lay forgotten among whins that never wanted bloom, and thick, soft, salty grass. Two plantings of tall trees kept the wind off, and the centre of it beaked in warm suns. It was like a garden standing out upon the sea, cut off from the throng road at all tides by a cluster of salt pools and an elbow of the Duglas Water.

Here the Sea-Fairy was always waiting for the girl, walking up and down in one or other of the tree-clumps. He had doffed his fine clothes after their first meeting for plain ones, and came douce and soberly, but aye with a small sword on his thigh.

The girl knew the folly of it; but to-morrow was always to be the last of it, and every day brought new wonders to her. He fetched her rings once, of cunning make, studded with stones that tickled the eye in a way the cairngorm and the Cromalt pearl could never come up to.

She would finger them as if they were the first blaeberries of a season and she was feared to spoil their bloom, and in a rapture the Sea-Fairy would watch the sparkle of eyes that were far before the jewels.

"Do your folk wear these?" she asked.

"Now and then," he would say, "now and then. Ours is a strange family: to-day we may have the best and the richest that is going, to-morrow who so poor, without a dud to our backs and a mob crying for our heads?"

"*Ochanorie!* They are the lovely rings any way."

"They might be better; they would need to be much better, my dear, to be good enough for you."

"For me!"

"They're yours – for a kiss or two," and he put out an arm to wind round the girl's waist.

Marseli drew back and put up her chin and down her brows.

"*Stad!*" she cried. "We ken the worth of fairy gifts in these parts. Your rings are, likely enough, but chuckie-stones if I could but see them. Take them back, I must be going home."

The little man took the jewels with a hot face and a laugh.

"Troth," he said, "and the same fal-fals have done a lover's business with more credit to them before this. There are dames in France who would give their souls for them – and the one they belong to."

"You have travelled?" said Marseli. "Of course a sea-fairy – "

"Can travel as he likes. You are not far wrong, my dear. Well, well, I ken France! O France, France! round and about the cold world, where's your equal?"

His eyes filled with tears, and the broadcloth on his breast heaved stormily, and Marseli saw that here was some sad thinking.

"Tell me of Fairydom," said she, to change him off so dull a key.

"'Tis the same, the same. France and fairyland, 'tis the same, self-same, madame," said the sea-prince, with a hand on his heart and a bow.

He started to tell her of rich and rolling fields, flat and juicy, waving to the wind; of country houses lost and drowned among flowers. "And all the roads lead one way," said he, "to a great and sparkling town. Rain or shine, there is comfort, and there is the happy heart! The windows open on the laughing lanes, and the girls lean out and look after us, who prance by on our horses. There is the hollow hearty hoof-beat on the causey stones; in the halls the tables gleam with silver and gold; the round red apples roll over the platter among the slim-stemmed wine-beakers. It is the time of soft talk and the head full of gallant thoughts. Then there are the nights warm and soft, when the open doors let out the laughing and the gliding of silk-shooned feet, and the airs come in heavy with the scent of breckan and tree!"

"On my word," said Marseli, "but it's like a girl's dream!"

"You may say it, black-eyes, *mo chridhe!* The wonder is that folk can be found to live so far astray from it. Let me tell you of the castles." And he told Marseli of women sighing at the harp for far-wandered ones, or sewing banners of gold. Trumpets and drums and the tall chevaliers going briskly by with the jingle of sword on heel on the highway to wars, every chevalier his love and a girl's hands warm upon his heart.

That night Marseli went early abed to wander in fairydom.

Next day the sea-gentleman had with him a curious harp that was not altogether a harp, and was hung over the neck by a ribbon.

"What hast here?" asked Marseli.

"A salve for a sore heart, lass! I can play on it some old tunes, and by the magic of it I'm back in my father's home and unafeared."

He drew his white fingers over the strings and made a thin twittering of music sweeter than comes from the *clarsach*-strings, but foreign and uncanny. To Marseli it brought notions of far-off affairs, half sweet, half sad, like the edges of dreams and the moods that come on one in loneliness and strange places, and one tune he played was a tune she had heard the French traffickers sing in the bay in the slack seasons.

"Let me sing you a song," said he, "all for yourself."

"You are bard?" she said, with a pleased face.

He said nothing, but touched on the curious harp, and sang to the girl's eyes, to the spark of them and the dance of them and the deep thought lurking in their corners, to her lips crimson like the rowan and curled with pride, to the set of breast and shoulder, and the voice melting on the tongue.

It was all in the tune and the player's looks, for the words were fairy to the girl, but so plain the story, her face burned, and her eyes filled with a rare confusion.

"'Tis the enchantment of fairydom," said she. "Am not I the *oinseach* to listen? I'll warrant you have sung the same to many a poor girl in all airts of the world?"

The little one laughed and up with the shoulders. "On my sword," quo' he, "I could be content to sing to you and France for all my time. Wilt come with a poor Prince on a Prince's honour?"

He kissed her with hot lips; his breath was in her hair; enchantment fell on her like a plaid, but she tore herself away and ran home, his craving following at her heels.

That night Marseli's brothers came to knives with the French traffickers, and the morning saw the black-avised ones sailing out over-sea for home. Back to French Foreland they came no more, and Finne-side took to its own brewing for lack of the red wine of France.

That, too, was the last of the Sea-Fairy. Marseli went to the Water-foot and waited, high tide and low; she cried the old child tune and she redded her hair, but never again the little man with the dainty clothes, and the sword upon his thigh.

Shudderman Soldier

BEYOND the Beannan is the Bog of the Fairy-Maid, and a stone-put farther is the knowe where Shudderman Soldier died in the snow. He was a half-wit who was wise enough in one thing, for he knew the heart of a maid, and the proof of it came in the poor year, when the glen gathered its corn in boats, and the potato-shaws were black when they burst the ground, and the catechist's horse came home by Dhuloch-side to a widow that reckoned on no empty saddle. And this is the story.

"Ho, ho, suas e!" said the nor' wind, and the snow, and the black frost, as they galloped down Glenaora like a leash of strong dogs. It was there was the pretty business! The Salachary hills lost their sink and swell in the great drifts that swirled on them in the night; the dumb white swathes made a cold harvest on the flats of Kilmune; the frost gripped tight at the throats of the burns, and turned the Salmon-Leap to a stack of silver lances. A cold world it was, sure enough, at the mouth of day! The blood-shot sun looked over Ben Ime for a little, and that was the last of him. The sheep lay in the shoulder of the hill with the drift many a crook's-length above them, and the cock-of-the-mountain and the white grouse, driven on the blast, met death with a blind shock against the edge of the larch-wood.

Up from Lochow, where Kames looks over to Cruachan, and Cruachan cocks his grey cap against Lorn, a foolish lad came that day for a tryst that was made by a wanton maid unthinking. Half-way over the hill he slipped on the edge of a drift, and a sore wound in the side he got against a splinter of the blue stone of the Quey's Rock; but he pushed on, with the blood oozing through his cut vest. Yet, in spite of himself, he slept beyond the Bog of the Fairy-Maid. *Mo-thruaigh! mo-thruaigh!* The Fairy-Maid came and covered him up close and warm with a white blanket that needs no posting, and sang the soft tune a man hears but once, and kissed him on the beard as he slept in the drift – and his name had been Ellar Ban.

Round by the king's good highroad came Solomon the carrier with his cart, and many a time he thought of turning between Carnus and Kilmune. But he was of the stuff of Clan Coll, and his mare was Proud Maisie. He had a boll of meal from Portinsherrich, from the son of a widow woman who was hungry in Inneraora and waiting for that same.

"No Ellar here yet!" he said at Kilmune when he asked, and they told him. "Then there's a story to tell, for if he's not here, he's not at Kames, and his grave's on the grey mountain."

Later came Luath, the collie of Ellar, slinking through the snow wet and weary, and without wind enough for barking. 'Twas as good as the man's ghost.

The shepherds came in from the fanks, and over from the curling at Carlonan, to go on a search.

Long Duncan of Drimfern, the slim swarthy champion, was there before them. He was a pretty man – the like never tied a shoe in Glenaora – and he was the real one who had Mairi's eye, which the dead fellow thought had the laugh only for him. But, lord! a young man with a good name with the shinty and the *clachneart* has other things to think of than the whims of women, and Donacha never noticed.

"We'll go up and see about it – about him at once, Mairi," he said, sick-sorry for the girl. All the rest stood round pitying, because her kists were said to be full of her own spinning for the day that was not to be.

Mairi took him to the other side of the peat-stack, and spoke with a red face.

"Is it any use your going till the snow's off the hill, Drimfern?" she said, biting at the corner of her brattie, and not looking the man in the face.

"*Dhia gleidh sinn!* it's who knows when the white'll be off the snouts of these hills, and we can't wait till – I thought it would ease your mind." And Donacha looked at the maid stupid enough. For a woman with her heart on the hill, cold, she was mighty queer on it.

"Yes, yes; but it's dangerous for you to go up, and the showers so heavy yet. It's not twenty finger-lengths you can see in front of you, and you might go into the bog."

"Is't the bog I would be thinking of, Mairi? It's little fear there is of that, for here is the man that has been on Salachary when the mist was like smoke, as well as when the spittle froze in my mouth. Oh, I'm not the one to talk; but where's the other like me?"

Mairi choked. "But, Dona – but, Drimfern, it's dead Ellar must be; and – and – you have a widow mother to mind."

Donacha looked blank at the maid. She had the sweet face, yon curve of the lip, and the soft turn of the neck of all Arthur's children, ripe of the cheek, with tossed hair like a fairy of the lake, and the quirk of the eye that never left a plain man at ease if he was under the threescore. There were knives out in the glen for many a worse one.

It was the lee of the peat-stack they stood in, and the falling flakes left for a while without a shroud a drop of crimson at the girl's feet. She was gripping tight at her left wrist under the cover of her apron till the nails cut the flesh. There was the stress of a dumb bard's sorrow in her face; her heart was in her eyes, if there had been a woman to see it; but Drimfern missed it, for he had no mind of the dance at the last Old New Year, or the ploy at the sheep-dipping, or the nuts they cracked on the hot peats at Hallowe'en.

The girl saw he was bound to go. He was as restless as if the snow was a swarm of *seangans*. She had not two drops of blood in her lips, but she tried to laugh as she took something out from a pocket and half held it out to him. He did not understand at first, for if he was smart on the *caman* ball, 'twas slow in the ways of women he was.

"It's daft I am. I don't know what it is, Donacha, but I had a dream that wasn't canny last night, and I'm afraid, I'm afraid," said the poor girl. "I was going to give you – "

Drimfern could not get the meaning of the laugh, strained as it was. He thought the maid's reason was wandering.

She had, whatever it was – a square piece of cloth of a woman's sewing – into the man's hand before he knew what she would be after; and when his fingers closed on it, she would have given a king's gold to get it back. But the Tullich lads, and the Paymaster's shepherd from Lecknamban, with Dol' Splendid and Francie Ro, in their plaids, and with their crooks, came round the gable-end. Luath, who knew Glenaora as well as he knew Creag Cranda, was with them, and away they went for the hill. All that Donacha the blind one said, as he put the sewing in his pocket to look at again, was, "Blessing with thee!" for all the world like a man for the fair.

Still the nor' wind, and the snow, and the dark frost said "*Suas e!*" running down the glen like the strong dogs on the peching deer; and the men were not a hundred yards away from the potato-pit when they were ghosts that went out altogether, without a sound, like Drimendorran's Grey Dame in the Red Forester's story.

A white face on a plump neck stood the sting of the storm dourly, though the goodwife said it would kill her out there, and the father cried "Shame!" on her sorrow, and her a maiden. "Where's the decency of you?" says he, fierce-like; "if it was a widow you were this day you couldn't show your heart more." And into the house he went and supped two cogies of brose, and swore at the *sgalag* for noticing that his cheeks were wet.

When the searchers would be high on the hill Shudderman came on the maid. He was a wizened, daft old one, always in a tinker Fencible's tartan trews and scarlet doublet. He would pucker his bare brown face like a foreign Italian, and whistle continually. The whistle was on his face when he came on the girl standing behind the byre, looking up with a corpse's whiteness where the Beannan should be.

"Te-he! Lord! but we're cunning," said the soldier. "It's a pity about Ellar, is it not, white darling?"

Mairi saw nothing, but swallowed a sob. Was this thing to know her secret, when the wise old woman of the glen never guessed it? There was something that troubled her in his look.

The wee creature put his shoulder against the peats, and shoved each hand up the other sleeve of his doublet while he whistled soft, and cunningly looked at the maid. The cords of her neck were working, and her breast heaved sore, but she kept her teeth tight together.

"Ay, ay, it's an awful thing, and him so fond, too," he went on; and his face was nothing but a handful of wrinkles and peat-smoke. It was a bigger ploy for the fool than a good dinner.

"What – who – who are you talking about, you poor *amadan?*" cried Mairi, desperately.

"Och, it's yourself that'll know. They're saying over at Tullich and up-by at Miss Jean's, Accurach, that it's a bonny pair you would make, you and Ellar. Yonnat Yalla says he was the first Lochow man ever she saw that would go a mile out of his way for a lass, and I saw him once come the round-about road by Cladich because it was too easy to meet you coming the short cut over the hill. Oh! there's no doubt he was fond, fond, and – "

"Amadan!" cried the maid, with no canny light in her eyes.

"Hoots! You're not angry with me, darling. I ken, I ken. Of course Drimfern's the swanky lad too, but it's not very safe this night on yon same hill. There's the Bog of the Fairy-Maid that never was frozen yet, and there's the Quey's Rock, and – te-he! I wouldn't give much for some of them not coming back any more than poor Ellar. It's namely that Drimfern got the bad eye from the Glenurchy woman come Martinmas next because of his taking up with her cousin-german's girl, Morag Callum."

"Yon *spàgachd* doll, indeed!"

"God, I do not know about that! but they're telling me he had her up at all the reels at Baldy Geepie's wedding, whatever, and it's a Maclean tartan frock she got for the same – I saw it with my own eyes."

"Lies, lies, lies," said the girl to herself, her lips dry, her hands and feet restless to do some crazy thing to kill the pain in her heart.

She was a little helpless bird in the hands of the silly one.

He was bursting himself inside with laughing, that couldn't be seen for the snow and the cracks on his face.

"But it's not marriages nor tartan you'll be thinking on, Mairi, with your own lad up there stiff. Let Morag have Drimfern – "

"You and your Morag! Shudderman, if it was not the crazy one you were, you would see that a man like Donacha Drimfern would have no dealings with the breed of MacCallum, tinker children of the sixty fools."

"Fools here or fools there, look at them in the castle at Duntroon! And Drimfern is – "

"Drimfern again! Who's thinking of Drimfern, the mother's big pet, the soft, soft creature, the poor thing that's daft about the shinty and the games – and – and – Go in-by, haverer, and – oh, my heart, my heart!"

"Cripple Callum," whistled the daft wee one; and faith it was the great sport he was having! The flame sparkled in the lass's eyes; she stamped furiously in the snow. She could have gone into the house, but the Shudderman would follow, and the devil was in him, and she might just as well tell her story at the cross-roads as risk. So she stayed.

"Come in this minute, O foolish one!" her mother came to the door and craved; but no.

The wee *bodach* took a wee pipe from his big poke and started at the smoking. When his match went out the dark was almost flat on the glen, and a night-hag complained with a wean's cry in the planting beyond the burn. At each draw of the pipe the eyes of the soldier glinted like a ferret's, and like any ferret's they were watching. He put in a word between-while that stabbed the poor thing's heart, about the shame of love in maids uncourted, and the cruelty of maids that cast love-looks for mischief. There were some old havers about himself here and there among the words: of a woman who changed her mind and went to another man's bed and board; of sport up the glen, and burials beyond; and Ellar Ban's widow mother, and the carry-on of Drimfern and the Glenurchy woman's cousin-german's girl. And it was all ravelled, like the old story Loch Finne comes up on the shore to tell when the moon's on Sithean Sluaidhe.

The girl was sobbing sore. "Man!" she said at last, "give me the peace of a night till we know what is" The *amadan* laughed at her, and went shauchling down to the cotter's, and Mairi went in out of the darkness.

The hours passed and passed, and the same leash of strong dogs were scouring like fury down Glenaora, and the moon looked a little through a hole, and was sickly at the sight, and went by in a hurry. A collie's bark in the night came to the house where the people waited round the peats, and "Oh, my heart!" said poor Mairi.

The father took the tin lantern with the holes in it, and they all went out to the house-end. The lantern-light stuck long needles in the night as it swung on the goodman's finger, and the byre and the shed and the peat-stack danced into the world and out of it, and the clouds were only an arm's length overhead.

The men were coming down the brae in the smother of snow, carrying something in a plaid. The dog was done with its barking, and there was no more sound from the coming ones than if they were ghosts. Like enough to ghosts they looked. No one said a word till the goodman spoke.

"You have him there?" he said.

"Ay, *beannachd leis!* all that there is of him," said the Paymaster's man; and they took it but an' ben, where Mairi's mother had the white dambrod cloth she had meant for herself, when her own time came, on the table.

"It's poor Ellar, indeed," said the goodman, noticing the fair beard.

"Where's Donacha? where's Drimfern?" cried Mairi, who had pulled herself together and come in from the byre-end, where she had waited to see if there was none of the watchers behind.

The Paymaster's man was leaning against the press-door, with a face like the clay; Dol' Splendid was putting a story in the *sgalag's* ear; the Tullich men were very busy on it taking the snow off their boots. Outside the wind had the sorry song of the curlew.

"Me-the-day! it's the story of this there is to tell," at last said Francie Ro, with a shake of the head. "Poor Drimfern – "

"Drimfern – ay, where's Drimfern in all the world?" said the goodman, with a start. He was standing before his girl to keep her from seeing the thing on the table till the wife had the boots covered. It was the face of a *cailleach* of threescore Mairi had.

"It's God knows! We were taking Ellar there down, turn about resting. It was a cruel business, for the drifts. There's blood on his side where he fell somewhere, and Drimfern had to put a clout on it to keep the blood off his plaid. That's Drimfern's plaid. When Donacha's second turn was over up at the bog, we couldn't get a bit of him. He's as lost as the deer the Duke shot, and we looked and whistled for hours."

The maid gave a wee turn to the door, shivered, and fell like a clod at her mother's feet.

"Look at yon, now! Am not I the poor father altogether?" said the old man with a soft lip to his friends. "Who would think, and her so healthy, and not married to Ellar, that she would be so much put about? You'll excuse it in her, lads, I know, for she's not twenty till the dipping-time, and the mother maybe spoiled her."

"Och, well," said the Splendid one, twisting his bonnet uneasy in his hands, "I've seen them daft enough over a living lad, and it's no great wonder when this one's dead."

They took the maid beyond to the big room by the kitchen, and a good mother's redding put her to rights. A search in the morning for Drimfern was set by the men. They had a glass before going home, and when they were gone the *bòchdans* came in the deep hollow of the night and rattled the windows and shook the door-sneck; but what cared yon long white thing on the goodwife's dambrod tablecloth?

At the mouth of day there was one woman with a gnawing breast looking about the glen-foot among the snow for the Shudderman soldier. She found him snedding the shaft of a shinny-stick at the Stronmagachan Gate, and whistling as if it was six weeks south of Whitsunday and the woods piping in the heat.

"I ken all about it, my white little lamb," he said with a soft speech. "All about them finding Ellar, and losing a better man, maybe, but any way one that some will miss more."

"God's heavy, heavy on a woman!" said the poor child. "I gave Donacha a sampler with something sewn on it yesterday, and the men, when they go up the hill to look for him to-day, will get it on him – and –

it would – "

"Ay, ay, ay! I ken, my dear. We'll put that right, or I'm no soldier." And the little man cocked his bonnet on his head like a piper. Then he was sorry for the pride of it, and he pulled it down on his face, and whistled to stop his nose from jagging.

"My heart! my bruised heart! they're saying sorry things of Ellar, and Donacha dead. The cotter's wife was talking this morning, and it'll send me daft!"

"Blind, blind" quo' the soldier; "but you'll not be shamed, if the *amadan* can help it."

"But what can you do, my poor Shudderman? And yet – and yet – there's no one between Carnus and Croitbhile I can speak to of it."

"Go home, white love, and I'll make it right," said the daft one, and faith he looked like meaning it.

"Who knows?" thought the girl. Shudderman was chief enough with the Glenurchy woman, and the Glenurchy woman sometimes gave her spells to her friends. So Mairi went home half comforted.

A cogie of brose and a bit braxy in his belly, and a farl of cake in his poke, and out stepped the Shudderman with never a word to any one about the end of his journey. Dol' Splendid had told him the story of the night before, and whereabout Drimfern was lost, close beyond the Beannan. He would find the body and the sampler, he promised himself as he plunged up the brae at Taravhdubh. The dogs were nearly as furious as the night before, and the day's eye was blear. Hours passed, and the flats of Kilmune were far below.

There was nothing in all the world but whiteness, and a silly old *bodach* with a red coat trailing across it. Shudderman Soldier sank his head between his shoulders as he pushed himself up with his hazel crook, his tartan trews in rags about his ankles, his doublet letting in the teeth of the wind here and there, and at the best grudging sore its too tight shelter for his shrunk body. He had not the wind to whistle, but he gasped bits of "Faill-il-o," and between he swore terribly at the white hares that jerked across in front of him with the ill-luck of a lifetime on their backs.

If it was the earth that was white, the sky was not far behind it; if they were paper, it would take schooling to write on them straight, for there wasn't a line between them. The long sweep of Balantyre itself was lost, and the Beannan stone was buried. The creature's brogues were clods of snow, ugly, big, without a shape: his feet were lumps of ice; his knees shook under his frail skinful of bones; but, by the black stones, 'twas the man's heart he had!

When the snow made a paste on his win'ard cheek, he had it off with a jerk of the head, and one of the jerks put off his bonnet. Its frozen ribbons had been whipping his eyes, and he left it where it fell, with never a glance over his shoulder. His hair clogged with flakes that kept the frost even after they fell. It was a peching effort for the foot of the Beannan brae.

"Poor lamb, poor Mairi, calf of my heart!" gasped the soldier to himself. He was staggering half blind through the smother of snow, now and then with a leg failing below him, and plunging him right or left. Once his knees shut like a gardener's gully, and he made a crazy heap in the drift. His tired wrists could hardly bring him up, and the corpse of the world swung in his eyes when he was on his feet again and trying to steady himself.

There's a green knoll beside the Bog of the Fairy-Maid, where the wee folks dance reels when the moon's on it, and there the old fellow struggled to. He thought if he was up there he would see some sign of what he wanted. Up he pushed, with the hazel *cromag* bending behind him, and his brogues slipping on the round snow-soles. Up he went, with the pluck of a whole man, let alone a poor silly object; up he went till he got his foot on the top, and then his heart failed, for he saw nothing of what he sought.

"I'll look again when I'm out of this foolish sleep, – I'll see better when I waken" said the poor *amadan*; and behold the dogs were on him! and he was a man who was.

For all that, the story tells, Drimfern was no ghost. When he was lost he found Kames, where the Callum girl was that came to his fire-end later and suckled his clan. And Ellar's mother, dressing her son's corpse in the house at Kilmune, found on his wound a sampler that went with him to his long home in green Inishail. Its letters, sewn in the folly of a woman, told her story: –

"Let him kiss me with the kisses of his mouth: for thy love is better than wine."

War

I

IT was the pause of the morning, when time stands, and night and day breathe hard ere they get to grips. A cock with a foggy throat started at the crowing, down at Slochd-a-Chubair. Over from Stron a shrewd thin wind came to make stir among the trees in the Duke's big garden, and the crows rasped their beaks on the beech-branches, for they knew that here was the day's forerunner. Still and on the town slept, stretched full out, dour set on the business. Its quirky lanes and closes were as black as the pit. There was only one light in all the place, and a big town and a bonny it is, house and house with high outside stairs and glass windows, so that the wonder is the King himself does not take thought to stay in it, even if it were only for the comfort of it and the company of the MacCailein Mor. Only one light, and that was splashing, yellow, and mixed with a thick peat-reek, out of Jean Rob's open door, facing the bay, on the left, on the Lowlands road. Now and then Jean would come to the door and stand, a blob of darkness in the yellow light, to see if the day was afoot on Ben Ime, or to throw a look at the front of the town for signs of folk stirring.

"Not a peep, not a peep! Sleep! sleep! Few of them part with a man to-day with so sore a heart as Jean Rob."

Then back to her Culross girdle, for she was at the baking of bannocks to go in her husband's *dorlach* for the wars.

She had not shut an eye all night. Rob snored at her side slow and heavy while she lay on her back on a bed of white hay, staring up at the black larch joists glinting with the red scad of the peats. She was a Crarae woman, and that same people were given to be throng with the head, and she kept thinking, thinking even on. At last she could bide it no longer, so she up with a leap on the floor to face a new day and all the luck of it.

About the luck being good or ill there might be little doubt. It was the year after they started at the building of the Castle, a laggard spring at the hind-end of a cruel winter, with not a fin in all the seas for the poor fishermen, and black mutton at six Saxon shillings the side. And what the wars were about Jean Rob or her like little knew or cared. Very little, like enough, as is the way with wars, but any way wars there were: the Duke and his House would have it that their people must up and on with belt and target, and away on the weary road like their fathers before them. Some said it was the old game with the Inverlochy dogs (rive them and seize them!); others, that some bastard was at variance with the Duke about the Papist Stewarts – a silly lad called Tearlach with a pack of wild Irishers and duddy Macleans and Macdonalds and Camerons from the Isles and the North at his back.

"Bundle and Go" it was any way in Campbell country from Cruachan to Cowal, from Cantyre to the march of Keppochan, and that's the fine rolling land of sappy grasses and thick woods. In the heart and midst of it Duke Archie played dirl on the boss of his shield on a cold March day, and before night swords were at the sharping from shore to shore. That's war for ye – quicker than flame, surer than word of mouth, and poor's the man who says "What for?" to his chief.

Rob Donn, for all that, was vassal to no man; for he was come of the swordsmiths of the glen, and they had paper to show that their rigs were held for no service other than beating out good fighting steel on the anvil. Poor as he was, he could wear one feather in his bonnet if his fancy was on feathers, and no one bragged more of his forefolk. But Elrigmor – a thin old man with little stomach for quarrels – offered twenty pounds English for a man to take his place with the Campbells; and Rob took the money and the loan of Elrigmor's sword, half for the sake of the money and half for the sake of a bit play with Sir Claymore.

Said he to his wife, jingling the Geordies in his hand on the day he got them, "Here's the price of a hero; and troth it's little enough for a good armsmith's blood!"

"Don't say it, Rob," said Jean.

"Och! I am but laughing at thee, goodwife. Brave dogs would they be that would face the tusks of the Diarmaid boars. Like the wind on the chaff – troosh! – we'll scatter them! In a week I'll be home."

"In a week?"

"To be sure, Jean. I'll buy with the money a stot or two on the road to bring back with me, for there's little lifting in the Duke's corps, more's the pity! My grandfather seldom came back from the wars without a few head of cattle before him."

So the money went in Rob Donn's sporran, and Jean would have bit her tongue out before she would crave for part o't from a man going among strangers and swords.

The bairn had but one word for her father from then till he started, and that was "Cockade" What it was the little one never knew, but that it was something braw and costly, a plaything for a father to go far off for.

"Two or three of them, my white love!" would Rob Donn say, fond and hearty. "They'll be as thick as nuts on the ground when we're done of the gentry that wear them on their bonnets." And he had a soft wet eye for the child, a weakling, white and thin, never quite the better of the snell winds of winter. If cockades, indeed, were to be had for the fighting of a fortnight without sleep, Rob Donn would have them for her.

So now was the morning to put on fighting gear and go on the foray for white cockades.

By-and-by a cruisie-light crept out at the gables of the town, and the darkness filled with the smell of new peat burning. Aora, spluttering past Jean Rob's door with a gulp into the Cooper's Pool, made, within the house, the only sound of the morning.

Jean scraped the meal off her hands and went again to the door to look about and listen.

"Ay, ay! up at last," she said to herself.

"There's the Major's light, and Kate Mhor up for the making of his breakfast, and a lowe in the weaver's shed. The Provost's is dark – poor man! – it's little his lady is caring!"

She was going to turn about and in, when the squeal of a bagpipe came from the townhead, and the player started to put his drones in order. "Ochan! ochan!" said poor Jean, for here, indeed, was the end of her hopes; there was no putting back from the Duke's errand. She listened a little to the tuning as if it was the finest of *piobaireachds*, and it brought a curious notion to her mind of the first reel she danced with her man to the squeezing of that same sheepskin. Then the reeds roared into the air of "Baile Inneraora."

"Och a Dhé'! siod e nis! Eirich, eirich, Rob!" she cried in to the man among the blankets, but there was no need for the summons. The gathering rang far ben in the chambers of sleep, and Rob was stark awake, with a grasp at his hip for the claymore.

"Troth! I thought it was the camp! and them on us," he laughed foolishly in his beard.

Up and down the street went Dol' Dubh, the Duke's second piper, the same who learned the art of music right well from the Macruimens of Boreraig, and he had as sweet a finger on the chanter as Padruig himself, with the nerve to go round the world. Fine, fine it was for him, be sure, to be the summoner to battle! Lights jumped to the little lozens of the windows and made streaks on the cracks of the doors, and the Major's man came from his loft ganting with a mouth like the glee'd gun, a lantern swinging on a finger, making for the stable to saddle his master's horse. A garret window went up with a bang, and Peter MacIntyre, wright, put out a towsy head and snuffed the air. It was low tide in the two bays, and the town was smelling less of peat-reek than of sea-wrack and saltness. One star hung in the north over Dunchuach.

"They have the good day for starting the jaunt, whatever," said the wright. "If I was a stone or two lighter, and had one to look after the shop, it's off on this ploy I would be too." He took in his head, the top nodding briskly on his Kilmarnock bonnet, and wakened the wife to help him on with his clothes.

> "Aora, Aora, Baile Inneraora
> I got a bidding to Baile Inneraora;
> I got the bidding, but little they gave me,
> Aora, Aora, Baile Chailein Mhoir !"

Dol' Dubh was up at the Cross, swelled out like a net-bow, blasting furiously, his heart athump with the piper's zest. Doors drummed, windows
screeched in their cases, women's voices went from land to land, and the
laugh and cry of bairns new roused from the hot toss of dreams. Far up the
highroad a horse's hoofs were dunting hollow and hearty on the stones,
and by-and-by through the Arches trotted the Cornal, his tall body straight
and black against the dun of the gables. He had a voice like a rutting deer.
"Master Piper," he roared to Dol' Dubh, tugging his beast back on its
haunches, "stop that braggart air and give us 'Bundle and Go,' and God
help the Campbell that's not on the Cadger's Quay before the sun's over
Stron Point!"

"Where is the air like it?" said Dol' to himself, slacking a reed with a
thumb-nail. "Well they ken it where little they love it with its vaunting!"
But he up with his drones on his shoulder and into the tune that had the
Cornal's fancy. Beside him the Cornal stood at his horse's stirrup in the
grey-brown of the morning, his head still light with the bottle of claret wine
his lady in Lecknamban had put before him ere he had boot over saddle.

Then the town stirred to its affairs. The Major's horse went clattering
over the cobble-stones to his door-end, the arm-room door opened, and
old Nanny Bheag, who kept the key, was lifted off her feet and in, on the
rush of young lads making for the new guns Lorne Clerk had up from the
Low Country. On the belts of the older men, loth to leave the fire-end,
mothers and wives were hanging bags with thick farls of cake, and cheese,
and the old Aora salve for sword-cuts. If they had their way of it, these *cailleachan,* the fighting gear would be all kebbucks of cheese and dry hose,
and no powder and ball. The men blustered, high-breasted, with big words
in their beards, and no name too dirty for the crew they were off to scatter
– praising themselves and making the fine prophecies, as their folks did
before them with better rights when the town was more in the way of going
to wars. Or they roundly scolded the weans for making noise, though their
eyes were learning every twist of the copper hair and every trick of the last
moment, to think on when long and dreary would be the road before them.

There was a break in Dol' Dubh's music, and high over the big town
rang the Cornal's voice, starting the bairns in their sleep and setting them
up and screaming.

"Laggards! laggards! O lazy ones! Out! out! Campbells before were
never so swear't to be marching. It is time to be steeping the withies!"

Hard back went the stout doors on the walls, and out ran the folk. The brogues skliffed and hammered; men with muskets, swords, dirks, and targes ran down the street, and women and children behind them. A tumult filled the town from side to side and end to end, and the lanes and closes were streaming with the light from gaping doors. Old and young, the boy and the snooded girl, women with bairn at breast, *bodach* and *cailleach*, took to the Cross muster, leaving the houses open to the wind and to the world. The cats thrummed by the fires, and the smell of the sea-wrack came in beside them.

"I have you here at last," said the Cornal, dour and dark, throwing his keen eyes along the row of men. "Little credit are ye to my clan and chief, and here's to the Lowlands low, and would to God I was there now among the true soldados with stomachs for slaughter and the right skill of fence and musketoon! A short tulzie, and a tow at the thrapple of bastard Chevalier would there be in that case. Here's but a wheen herds, weavers, and gillies holding Brown Betty like a kail-runt!"

He was one of the Craignish Campbells, the Cornal – Dugald, brother of Lachan who got death at a place called Fontenoy in the summer before – very sib to the duke, and it behoved the town-men to say nothing. But they cursed his eyes to each other on the corners of their mouths, and if he knew it he had sense enough to say nothing.

The women and bairns and the old folks stood in a great crowd behind the Cornal's horse. The Major's mare with him in the sell was dancing an uncanny spring near the Arches, full of freshness and fine feeding as a battle-horse should be, but overly much that way for a man sixteen finger-lengths round the belly and full of fish and ale. From Glen Beag came the slow morning, gusty and stinging; Stob-an-Eas stood black against the grey of it; the tide stretched from shore to shore unfriendly and forlorn.

Jean Rob, with the bairn at her brattie-string, was with the other women seeing her man away, stupid with two sorrows – one because he was going, and the other because he had twenty pounds in his sporran that he might well be doing without; for he was leaving the woman without a groat, and only a boll of meal in the girnel and a wee firkin of salted fish.

The steady breeze came yet from Stron, and sat snug in the sails of the six boats that carried the Duke's men over to Cowal. Brog-and-Turk's skiff put out first, himself at the helm in his tarry jacket; the others, deep down followed close on her heels. One by one they fell off from the quay. The men waved their bonnets and cried cheerily and vaunting, as was aye the good grace of Clan Diarmaid at the first and the last of forays.

"Blessings with ye!" cried the folk left behind, wet-eyed; and even the Provost's wife took a grief at her inside to see her man with a shaking lip look round the sail of the hin'most boat. Cheering and weeping, singing and *ochain!* there they were on the quay and on the sea, our own folk, our dear folk; and who were ever like them when it came to the bit, and stout hearts or kind hearts were wanted?

"Stand back, kindred!" cried the Cornal, putting spurs to his horse, and he pranced up the town-head, a pretty man, to join the Major and gallop round the loch-head to join the corps at Cairn-dubh.

Dol' Dubh stopped his playing at the bow of Brog-an-Turk's skiff when she gulped the first quaich of brine, and the men in all the boats started to sing the old boat-song of "Aora Mo Chridhe tha mi seoladh" –

> "Aora, my heart, I am sailing, sailing,
> Far to the South on the slope of the sea;
> Aora *mo chridhe*, it is cold is the far land,
> Bitter the stranger with wands on his doorway.
> Aora Mochree!"

It came back on the wind with a sorrow to break hearts, sinking and swelling as the wind took the fancy, and the long-necked herons stood on the fringe of the tide with their heads high to listen. The sails got scattered and shrunk, and the tune got thin and low, and lost at last in the swish of the waves on the shore, and the ears of those who listened heard the curlew piping cursedly loud over the Cooper's Pool. A grey cold day with rain on the tail of it. High Creag Dubh with its firs and alders and rowans stark and careless over the hollow town. Broad day and brightness, and the cruisies and candles burning the ghosts of flame in the empty houses, with doors wide to the empty street and the lanes and closes!

II

THE wanderer has ever the best of it, and wae wae are the hearts behind! Is it for war or sport, or for the red gold, that a man turns heel on his home and takes the world for his pillow? In his pack is the salve for care as well as for sword-cuts, for ever and always are new things happening. The road crooks through the curious glens; the beasts trot among the grass and fern and into the woods; the girls (the dear ones, the red-lipped ones!) come from the milking of the white-shouldered cattle and look with soft black eyes as he passes, and there is a new tale at the corner of every change-house fire. All that may befall a packman; but better's the lot of the fighter with steel at his haunch, fire at his heart, and every halt a day closer to them he would be seeking.

But the folks behind in the old place! *Mo thruaigh! mo thruaigh!* Daybreak, and hot sun, and the creeping in of the night, when the door must be snecked on the rover; the same place, and still with a want in it, and only guessing at where and how is the loved one out on strange ways on the broad world.

Far up the long Highlands the Campbells were on their way. Loch Sloy and Glen Falloch, Rannoch's bleakness and Ben Alder's steepness, and each morning its own wet grass and misty brae, and each night its dreams on the springy heather.

A woman was weeping on Achadunan because that her man was gone and her chimney stone was cold, and Rob Donn's sporran was emptied at her feet, though he knew not so much as the name of her. But he took a thought and said, "I'll keep the half, for long's the way before us, and ill is travelling among strangers without a roundpiece in the purse." That was but a day's march from Jean Rob, and she was making a supper of crowdie that was the first meal of the day.

On Spey-side was the camp of the Argylls, and card-play round the fires, with the muskets shining, and the pipes playing sweeter for slumber than for rouse.

"I will put my watch on this turn," said a black Lowlander in the heat of the game.

"Rob Donn's watch is the sun on Tom-an-uardar," said our hero, "but here are ten yellow Geordies," and out went his fortune among the roots of the gall.

"*Troosh! beannachd leat!*" and the coin was a jingle in the other one's pouch.

"I have plenty more where it came from, and cattle enough forbye," said our braggart, and he turned on his elbow whistling "Crodh Chailein."

But let them follow the drum who will, for us the story's beside the hearth. It is not a clatter of steel and the tulzies of Chevaliers, but the death of an only bairn.

In her house on the Lowlands road Jean Rob starved with the true Highland pride, that set a face content against the world at kirk or market. Between her and a craving stomach lay but shell-fish and herbs, for she had not a plack to spend, and the little one got all the milk that came from Mally, the dappled one, drying up for calving. Break of day would see the woman, white, thin, keen-eyed, out on the ebb before the fishing-boats were in, splashing in the pools in the sand for partans and clabbie-doos, or with two ready fingers piercing the sand to pull the long spout-fish from his hiding. Or she would put little stakes in the sand, and between them a taut line with baited hooks to coax the fish at high tide. But ill was her luck, indeed, for few were the fish that came to the lure to be lifted again at ebb.

Above Kilmalieu on the sea side of Dunchuach, in the tangle and dark of the trees, among the soft splashing soil, the wild leeks gave a scent to the air. These would Jean gather, and the nettle too, and turn them to thin broth; but that same was no fare for a Crarae stomach.

At night when the wee one slept, the mother would have her plaid on her head, and through the town, barefoot, in the darkness, passing the folk at the close-mouths quickly for fear they would speak to her, and her heart would crave for share of the noble supper that made steam from the door of her cousin the rich merchant.

Like a ghost sometimes, wandering about the Cadger's Quay or the gutting-stools, where she would be looking for a dropped giley or a hake from the nets, she would come on a young woman.

"*Dhé!* Jean Rob! is it thyself that is here?"

"Just Jean, my darling, for a little turn, because of the stir in the town, and the smell of the barking nets. Well I like the smell of the bark, and the wind takes little of it up the Lowlands road."

"Thou art not coming out much since the men went to the North. Art well at the house – the little one, now, bless her?"

"Splendid, splendid, m' *eudail*. Faith, it is too fat we will be getting on the fortune Rob got from Elrigmor."

"Indeed, yes, Jean, it was the great luck! When a poor person comes — "

"Hut tut! Poor nor rich, my people had their own place on Lochowside, and little did my Rob need MacNicol's dirty money; but he was aye fond of a 'horoyally,' and that's the way of his being among them."

"Well, well, if that's the way, our own people were good enough on a time; but a pedigree, thou wilt allow, is a poor plaster for a pain in the stomach. For me, I would have a good shaking of herring and money in the town. It was but black brochan for our one meal to-day, and my mother poorly."

"My dear! *och*, my dear! and I to brag of plenty! Little enough, in truth, is on my own board; but I have a boiling of meal if you come for it in the morning."

"Kindly, kindly, thou good dame. It would be but a loan."

"Yes, indeed, one will be running out of the wherewithal now and again, and 'twas aye. 'Mine is yours and yours is mine' in Gaeldom. But I must be stepping."

And while Jean Rob starved, there was never a word from the best and bravest off at the wars, or how they fared, only now and then a half tale from a travelling caird or a Low-Country carrier about gatherings and skirling pipes and hard knocks. His Grace himself kept a horse or two and a good rider on the other side of the Rest, to gallop hot-hoof into the Castle with the first news of how his clan won; but weary was the waiting.

The town took to its old appearance, the aged men clack-clacking with the shuttle, the boys scattering seed over the rig-and-fur of the ploughed fields, the women minding their houses. And that, too, is war for ye! The dirk is out, the brogues trail over the hills and through the glens, the clans meet and clash, the full heart belches blood, the grass soaks, the world and the chance of it is put on the luck of a swinging stroke at yon one's neck. War! war! red and lusty – the jar of it fills the land! But oh, *mo chridhe!* home in Glen Shie are women and bairns living their own day's life, and the crack will be blithe in the sheilings to come, for all your quarrels. Where is Hector, and where is Gilean-of-the-Axe, and where is Diarmaid of the boar's snout? They are all gone but for an old song at the sheiling-fire, and life, love, and the Fell Sergeant still come and go in the place the warriors made such stir in!

A stranger would think there was little amiss in the Duke's town. The women sang their long songs of love and yore as they span about the wheel and carded the wool; the bairns guddled in Jumping John's burn, and tore their kilts among the whins, and came home with the crows, red-faced and hungry-wamed. At the ale-house there was traffic by day, and heavy drovers and gaugers stamped their feet to the choruses at night. The day lengthened, and comforting winds came from the two bonny black glens; the bracken put on new growths, like the crook of St Molach that's up-by in the Castle; Easachosain reeled to the piping of birds.

There might be an eye many times a day on the Stron Point to see if a horseman was rounding it, and the cruisies were kept burning a little longer at night in case the news would come in the darkness like the Athol thieves. But patience was ever the gift of the Gael, and few lost heart.

And at last the news came of Culloden Moor.

It was on a Sunday – a dry clear day – and all the folk were at the church, with old Colin the minister sweating at it for the good of the Ceannloch fishermen in the loft. He was in the middle of his prayer when a noise came over the town, a dunting of hoofs on the causey of the Provost's house-front.

"Amen!" said the cunning Colin, quick as could be, and then, "Friends, here is news for us," and down the pulpit steps he ran briskly like a lad of twenty.

Peter MacIntyre set back the bolt from the door with a bang, and past him the people made rush. The Duke's rider from over the Rest was there in the saddle of a grey garron foaming at the mouth and its hurdies in a tremble.

"Your tidings, your tidings, good man!" cried the people.

The lad sat stark in the saddle, with his eyes wet and his nose pricking with the Gaelic pride.

"I have been at the Castle, and – "

"Your news, just man."

"I have been at the Castle, and MacCailein Mor, who said I rode well from the Rest, said I might come in-by and carry my budget to you."

"Out with it, Paruig, little hero. Is't good or ill?"

"What would it be, my heroes, with our own lads, but good? Where's the beat of them? It's 'The Glen is Mine' Dol' Dubh will be playing this day on Culloden, for ours is the battle. They scattered the dirty Northmen and the Irishers like chaff, and Cailein Mor himself gave me a horn of ale from his own hands on the head o't."

A roar went up that stirred the crows on Scaurnoch, and there was a Sunday spoiled for you; for the ale went free and merry in the change-house at the Duke's charge till the moon was over Ben Ime.

But there were five houses with the clocks stopped (for the ghosts take no heed of time); five houses with the glasses turned face to the wall (for who dare look in glass to see a wraith at the back of the shoulder?); there were four widows and five mothers wet faced, keening for five fine men who had been, and whose names were now writ on paper on the church door.

III

DAY followed day, and still home came no Campbells. They were far to the dreary North, plying sword and fire among the bad clans, harrying for the glory of MacCailein Mor.

And at last on a day the sea-pigs rolled and blew off Stron Point, and the scarts dived like arrows from the sun's eye, deep into a loch boiling with fish. Night found the brown sails bellying out on the scudding smacks, and the snouts of skiff and galley tearing the waves to get among the spoil. Bow-to-back, the nets spotted Finne mile on mile; the kind herrings crowded thick into them; the old luck was back, and the quays in the morning heard the fine tune of the cadger's clinking silver. In a hurry of hurries the fleet came up to the mouth of Shira – Tarbert men, Strathlachlan men, Minard men, black fellows from MacCallum country, and the wine-traffickers from French Foreland to swap sour claret for the sweet fat fish.

It was ho-ro! and spill the bicker in yon town, for all that the best of its men were away and afar at the killing. The smoke was black from the fires in the Cooper's Pool, the good healthy smell of the gut-pots sought up to the Castle door. Little doubt his Grace *(beannachd leis!)* would come out to the doorstep and curse because it made him bock his breakfast, dainty man!

Throng though the town was, round about the little house on the left of the Lowlands Road crept a queer quietness. The cow had dried, and the dull weather kept the spout fish too deep down in the sand for the ready fingers to reach them. So the household of Rob Donn starved to the bone.

"To-morrow – they will be home to-morrow," said Jean to herself every day to keep up her heart; but the days went by, and though it was something to know that Rob was not among the killed at Culloden, it was not something to stay the stomach. A stone-throw off were the best and kindest hearts in the world: the woman's cousin, the rich merchant, would give all he had on his board if he knew her trouble, and friends without number would share the last bite with her. But to ask it would be to say she was at the lowest, and to tell that Rob had left her nothing, and she would sooner die in her pride.

Such people as passed her way – and some of them old gossips – would have gone in, but the withie was aye across the door, and that's the sign that business is doing within no one dare disturb. The withie was ever there except at night, when Jean was scouring the countryside for something to eat.

The bairn dwined so fast that even the mother (and blind indeed's the mother at that bit) saw a little of it. There was no longer the creepie-stool at the back of the house, in the sun, and the bairn on it, watching the birds; her shanks grew thin like spirtles; her eyes sank far ben in her face, and she would not go the length of the door. She sat at the fireside and laughed her poor cold laugh less every day, till one long thought came to her that kept her busy at the thinking from morning till night with a face like a *cailleach* of eighty.

"White love, white love," Jean would be saying, "your father is on the road with stots and a pouch of cockades."

At that the bairn would come back from her roaming; but soon she was off again into the deeps of mind, her wide eyes like the windows of an empty house for all that could be seen through them.

"Oh! but it will be the fine cockade," poor Jean would press – "what am I saying? – the pack of your father will be full of them. Not the white ones of silk only, but the red and the grassy green, my little calf. You'll be wearing them when you will."

No heeding in the bairn's face.

Then Jean would go out and pull the tansy at the door, and give it to the little one to get the fine scent. The curious shells from the shore, too, would she gather, and lay in rings about the chair, and call her the Queen in her castle. For ever would there be a song at her lips, even if the drops would be in her eyes – old daft songs from fairs and weddings, and fairy rhyming and cheery stories about the Good People up on Sithean Sluaidhe. Her fingers were for ever soft about the bairn, her flesh and blood, stroking in the hair, softening the cushion, petting her in every hand's-turn. She made a treat to herself by asking her, now and then, something that had to be answered "Yes" or "No," and "Mother" was so sweet in her ears that she would be content to hear no more in all her lifetime.

All the day the bairn crouched up in a hoop-chair with her neck slack and her chin on her breast. Jean was loth to leave her in her bed in the mornings, for she had a notion that to get her out of the blankets and to put her in the clothes of the busy world would be to keep her in trim for living on.

Still there was no sign of the men returning. Often was Jean's foot at the door and her hand over her eyes to see if there was no stir at Stron or Kilachatrine, and but for good stuff, her heart failed five-score times a-day.

At last, on a day of days, the bairn could not be stirred to notice anything. The tansy fell out of her fingers, and she picked at the wool of the plaid that wrapped her; the shells had no charm for her eye.

Jean made the pack of the coming father as routh as a magic cave. "That father of yours, darling, what a many wonderful things he will bring! I see him on the road. Stots, and cows with milk brimming from the udders, and a pet sheep for his *caileag bheag;* pretty gold and silver things, and brooches and shining stuff. That father of yours! Hurry, father, hurry! Jingling things, and wee fairy-men, and bells to ring for you, m' *eudail;* pretty glasses and dishes to play with, and – O my darling! my darling!"

The bairn's face lost the deep red spots; her little mouth slacked and fell, her eyes shut on the sight of the fine things her poor mother made for her out of a rich and willing mind.

Jean lifted her and put her on the bed, and ran with a gutting-knife to where Mally the dappled one lay at the back.

"I must be doing it!" said the woman, and she bled the brute as they do in the poor years in Lorn, and took the cogie of blood into the house to make a pudding of. The last handful of meal in the girnel went into the pot with the warm blood, and she was stirring it with a spoon over the fire when the child cluttered at the throat.

Jean turned about with a cry, and at the minute a bagpipe's lilting came over the glassy bay from Stron Point.

It was Clan Campbell back from the wars, the heroes! clouted about the heads and with stains on their red waistcoats that were thicker than wine makes. Dol' Dubh played the old port, sweet and jaunty, at the head of them; the Cornal and the Major snuffed the herrings and said "Here's our own place, sure enough! See the smoke from our own peats! And the fine cock of the cap on Dunchuach!"

On the Lowlands road the town emptied itself, and the folks ran fast and furious – the boys first, the young women next, and the old folks peching behind. But if the town was up on the warriors soon, the Duke himself was before it. He saw the first of the Company from the Castle, and he was in the saddle for all his threescore, like a boy, and down like the wind to Boshang Gate.

"Halt!" cried the Cornal to his men, and Dol' Dubh's bag emptied itself with a grunt.

"Tha sibh an so! You are here, cousin," said the Duke. "Proud am I to see you and our good lads. They did the old trick well!"

"They did that, MacCailein. The stuff's aye to the fore."

"It's in the blood, man. We have't in us, high or low. I have but one thing to vex me."

"Name it, cousin."

"Well ye ken, Cornal. It's that I had not been with you to see the last crushing Clan Campbell may need to give to an asp's head."

"It was a good ploy missed, I'll not deny."

"What about the Tearlach one? Well plucked, they are telling me?"

"As foolish a lad as ever put tartan on hip, my lord! Frenchy, Frenchy, MacCailein! all outside and no cognisance. Yourself or any of your fore-bears at the head of his clans could have scoured all Albainn of Geordie's Low Country red-coats, and yet there were only six thousand true Gaels in all the fellow's corps."

"To read my letters, you would think the whole North was on fire!"

"A bantam's crow, cousin. Clan Campbell itself could have thrawed the neck of it at any time up to Dunedin."

"They made a fair stand, did they not?"

"Uch! Poor eno' – indeed it was not what you would call a coward's tulzie either."

"Well, well, that's over, lads! I am proud of my clan and town. *Slochd a Chubair gu bragh!* Stack your guns in the arm-room, see your wives and bairns, and come up-by to the Castle for the heroes' bite and sup. Who's that with the white cockade in his bonnet? Is't Rob Donn?"

"It is Rob Donn, cousin, with a bit of the ribbon contrivance for the diversion of his bairn. He tore it from the bonnet of the seventh man he put an end to."

"There's luck in the number, any way, though it was a dear plaything. March!"

Down the road, with their friends hanging about them, and the boys carrying guns and knapsacks, went the men for the town, and Rob Donn left the company as it passed near his door.

"Faith! 'tis a poor enough home-coming, without wife or bairn to meet one," said he, as he pushed in the door.

"Wife! wife!" he cried ben among the peat-reek, "there's never a stot, but here's the cockade for the little one!"

A Fine Pair of Shoes

THE beginnings of things are to be well considered – we have all a little of that art; but to end well and wisely is the gift of few. Hunters and herds on the corri and the hill – they are at the simple end of life, and ken the need for the task complete. The stag must be gralloched ere ye brag of him, the drove must be at the market ere ye say anything of the honesty of the glens ye pass through.

And what I like best about our own Gaels is their habit of bringing the work of a day or the work of a lifetime to what (in their own notions) is an end round and polished.

When our women die, they do it with something of a daintiness. Their dead-clothes are in the awmrie; I have seen them with the cakes toasted and the board set for their funerals. Travelling wide on unfriendly foreign roads, living by sword or wit, you know that our men, the poorest among them, with an empty sporran, kept the buttons of their duds of good silver, to pay, if need be, for something more than a gangrel's burial. I like to think of him in story who, at his end in bed, made the folk trick him out in gallant style with tartan, targe, brogue, and bonnet, and the sword in his hand.

"A Gaelic gentleman," said he, "should come to his journey's end somewhat snod and well-put-on." And his son played "Cha till mi tuilidh" ("I return no more") on the bagpipe by his firm command.

It is not even in this unco undertaking of Death that the polish must be put on the task (though poor's the creature who dies clumsily); it should be the same with every task of a day.

And so Baldi Crom, making a fine pair of shoes on a day in Carnus, put the best skill of his fingers to every stitch. He had been working at them since the command came in the morning, and now it was the mouth of night, and on one of them the finest of the fine sewing was still to do. About the place there was nobody but the old man, for he was the last, in a way, of the old stock of Carnus (now *a larach* of low lintels, and the net-tle over all) ; and he was without woman to put *caschrom* to his soil or hip to a creel of peats. And so he lived on the brae of Carnus – that same far up and lonely in the long glen.

"They'll be the best I ever put brog in," said he, looking fondly at the fine work, the yellow thread standing out on the toes, patterned like a leaf of the whortleberry, set about with the serpent-work of the old crosses. Bite nor sup, kail nor crowdie, did he taste all day. Working in the light of his open door, he could see, if he had the notion, the whole glen rolled out before him, brimming with sun, crossed in the heat of the day by deer from Dalavich seeking for the woods of Loch Finne; the blue reek of the townships at the far end might have cheered him with the thought that life was in sight though his house was lonely. But crouped over the lapstone, he made love to his work, heeding nothing else but the sewing of the fine pair of shoes.

It was the night before the town market. Droves of bellowing cattle – heifers, stots, and stirks – were going down the glen from Port Sonachan, cropping hurried mouthfuls by the way as they went and as the dogs would let them. And three Benderloch drovers came off the road and into Baldi Crom's house, after the night was down on the glen and he had the cruisie lighted. They sat them down round the fire in the middle of the floor and ate bannocks and cheese.

"How's thy family, 'Illeasbuig?" said a drover, stirring up the peat as if he were at his own door-end. Down on the roadside the cattle, black and yellow, crushed the sappy grass and mourned in bellows for their lost fields.

"Splendid! splendid!" said the old man, double over his shoes, fondling them with the fingers of a mother on a first baby. The light was low in the cruisie, for the oil was well down, and the fire and the cruisie made a ring of light that could scarcely slip over the backs of the men sitting round the peats. A goat scratched his head but-and-ben against the wattles; in corners the darkness was brown and thick.

"I hear Cailen's in the Low Country, but what has come of Tormaid?" said one, with knee-breeches, and hose of coarse worsted.

The old man gave a quick start, and the lapstone fell from his knees, the shoe he was at with it. He bent over and felt like a blind man for them on the floor before he made answer.

"Tormaid, my gallant son! Ye have not heard of him lately, then?"

"Never a word, 'Illeasbuig. People on the going foot, like drovers, hear all the world's gossip but the *sgeuls* of their own *sgireachd*. We have been far North since Martinmas: for us there must be many a story to tell 'twixt here and Inneraora. A stout lad and pretty, Tormaid too, as ever went to the beginning of fortune! Where might he be enow?"

"Here and there, friend, here and there! A restless scamp, a wanderer, but with parts. Had he not the smart style at the game of *camanachd*? He was namely for it in many places."

"As neat a player as ever took shinty in hand, master! I have the name of a fair player myself, but that much I'll allow your lad. Is he to the West side, or farther off?"

"Farther off, friend. The pipes now – have you heard him as a player on the chanter?"

"As a piper, 'Illeasbuig! His like was not in three shires. I have heard him at reel and march, but these were not his fancy: for him the *piobaireachds* that scholarly ones play!"

"My gallant boy!" said Baldi Crom, rubbing soft on the shoe with the palm of a hand.

"Once upon a time," said the drover, "we were on our way to a Lowland Tryst. Down Glen Falloch a Soccach man and I heard him fill the nightfall with the 'Bhoilich' of Morar, with the brag of a whole clan in his warbling. He knew piping, the fellow with me, and the tear came to his cheek, thinking of the old days and the old ploys among the dirks and *sgians.*"

"There was never the beat of him," said the shoemaker.

"Throughither a bit – "

"But good, good at heart, man! With a better chance of fortune he might be holding his head to-day as high as the best of them."

The drovers looked at each other with a meaning that was not for the eyes of the old man; but he had small chance of seeing it, for he was throng at his fine pair of shoes.

"He had a name for many arts," said the man with coarse hose, "but they were not the arts that give a lad settlement and put money in his purse."

"The hot young head, man! He would have cured," said the old man, sewing hard. "Think of it," said he: "was ever a more humoursome fellow to walk a glen with? His songs, his stories, his fast jump at one's meaning, and his trick of leaving all about him in a good key with themselves and him. Did ever one ask a Saxon shilling from his purse that it was not a cheery gift if the purse held it?"

"True, indeed!" said the drovers, eating bannocks and cheese.

"'Twixt heaven and hell," said the fellow with the coarse hose, "is but a spang. It's so easy for some folk to deserve the one gate – so many their gifts – that the cocksureness leaves them careless, and they wander into the wrong place."

"You were speaking?" said Baldi, a little angry, though he heard but half.

"I said thy son was a fellow of many gifts," answered the drover, in a confusion.

"He had no unfriends that I ken of," said the old man busy at the shoes; "young or old, man or woman."

"Especially woman," put in another drover, wrinkling at the eyes.

"I've had five sons: three in the King's service, and one in the Low Country; here's my young wanderer, and he was – he is – the jewel of them all!"

"You hear of him sometimes?"

"I heard of him and from him this very day," said Baldi, busy at the brogues, white and drawn at the face and shaking at the lips. "I have worked at these shoes since morning, and little time is there to put bye on them, for at Inneraora town must they be before breakfast. Solomon Carrier, passing at three, gives me a cry and takes them."

"They're a fine pair of shoes."

"Fine indeed; the finest of the fine! They're for a particular one."

"Duke John himself, perhaps?"

"No, man; a particular one, and were they not his in time a sorry man was I. They're the best Baldi Crom ever put leather on."

Till the turn of the night the drovers slept in their plaids, their cattle steaming out-by in the dark, munching the coarse grass selvedge, breathing heavy. And when the men and their beasts went in the darkness of the morning, Baldi Crom was still throng at his fine pair of shoes.

"I'm late, I'm surely late," said he, toiling hard, but with no sloven-work, at his task.

The rain had come with the morning, and was threshing out-by on peat and thatch. Inside, the fire died, and the cruisie gave warnings that its oil was low, but Baldi Crom was too throng on the end of his task to notice. And at last his house dropped into darkness.

"Tormaid! Tormaid! my little hero – I'm sore feared you'll die without shoes after all," cried the old man, staggering to the door for daylight. He had the door but opened when he fell, a helpless lump, on the clay floor. The rain slanted on his grey hairs and spat on a fine shoe.

Far down the good long glen the drovers were tramping after their cattle, and the dun morning was just before them when they got to the gate of Inneraora. Here there was a great to-do, for the kind gallows stood stark before the Arches. Round about it were the townspeople waiting for a hanging.

"Who is't, and what is't for?" asked the drover with the knee-breeches and the coarse hose, pushing into the crowd.

"Tormaid, the son of the Carnus cobbler," said a woman with a plaid over her head. "He killed a man in a brawl at Braleckan and raped his purse. Little enough to put tow to a pretty lad's neck for, sure enough!"

"Stand clear there!" cried a sharp voice, and the hang-man and his friend came to the scaffold's foot with a lad in front of them, his hands shackled behind his back. He was a strong straight lad, if anything overly dour in the look, and he wore a good coat and trews, but neither boot nor bonnet. Under the beam he put back his shoulders with a jerk and looked at the folk below, then over at Dunchuach with the mist above the fort like smoke.

"They might have given him a pair of old bauchels, if no better, to die in," said the drover in the woman's ear.

"*Ochanoch!* and they might!" she said. "The darling! He lost his shoes in swimming Duglas Water to get clear, and they say he sent yesterday to his father for a pair, but they're not come. Queer, indeed, is that, for 'twas the brag of the folks he came of that they aye died with a good pair of shoon on their feet!"

Castle Dark

YOU know Castle Dark, women?

"Well, we know the same, just man and blind!"

And you, my lads?

"None better, Paruig Dall; morning and night, in the moon and in the full white day!"

Then of Castle Dark is my story. Is the cruisie alight on the rafter? More peats, little one, on the fire.

Once upon a time Castle Dark was a place of gentility and stirring days. You have heard it, – you know it; now it is like a deer's skull in Wood Mamore, empty, eye-less, sounding to the whistling wind, but blackened instead of bleached in the threshing rains. When the day shines and the sun coaxes the drowsy mists from the levels by the river, that noble house that was brisks up and grey-whitens, minding maybe of merry times; the softest smirr of rain – and the scowl comes to corbie-stone and gable; black, black grow the stones of old ancient Castle Dark! Little one, *m' eudail*, put the door to, and the sneck down.

"True for you, Paruig Dall; you know the place as if you had seen it."

With eyes Paruig Dall has never seen it. But my friends tell me what they know, and beyond I have learned of myself. Up the river-side, many a time I pass to the place and over its low dykes, dry-stone, broken and crumbling to the heel. The moss is soft on the little roads, so narrow and so without end, winding round the land; the nettle cocks him right brag-gardly over the old home of bush and flower, poisoning the air. Where the lady dozed in her shady seat below the alder-tree, looking out between half-shut eyes at the proud Highlands – loch, glen, and mountain – is but a root rotten, and hacked by the woodman's whittle. A tangle of wild wood, bracken, and weed smothers the rich gardens of Castle Dark.

"It is so, it is so, Paruig Dall, blind man, prince among splendid pipers and storied men!"

And to stand on the broad clanging steps that lifted from the hunting-road to the great door – that is a thinking man's trial. To me, then, will be coming graveyard airs, yellow and vexatious, searching eager through my bones for this old man's last weakness. "Thou sturdy dog!" will they be saying, "some day, some day! Look at this strong tower!" With an ear to the gap on the side of the empty ditch, I can hear the hollowness of the house rumbling with pains, racked at *cabar* and corner-stone, the thought and the song gone clean away. There is no window, then, that has not a complaint of its own; no loophole, no vent, no grassy chimney that the blind fellow cannot hear the pipe of. Straight into the heart's core of Castle Dark looks the sun; the deep tolbooth of the old reivers and the bed-chamber of the maid are open wide to the night and to the star!

"*Ochan! ochan!*"

You that only ken the castle in common day or night and plain man's weather have but little notion of its wonders. It was there, and black and hollow, ere ever you were born, or Paruig Dall. To see Castle Dark one must take the Blue Barge and venture on two trips.

"The Blue Barge, just man?"

That same. The *birlinn ghorm*, the galley of fairy Lorn. It lies in the sunlight on the bay, or the moonlight in certain weathers, and twelve of the handsomest sit on the seats with the oars in their hands, the red shirt bulging over the kilt-belt. At the stern of the barge is the chair of the visitor. Gentle or semple, 'tis the same boat and crew, and the same cushioned chair, for all that make the jaunt to Castle Dark. My story is of two trips a man made by Barge Blue up the river to the white stairs.

He roved round the Lowlands road on a fine summer day, and out on the sands among the running salt threads of ebb tide. Among the shells, his eyes (as it might be) fell on the castle, and he had a notion to make the trip to it by a new road. Loudly he piped to sea. If loudly he piped, keen was the hearing, for yonder came the galley of fairy Lorn, the twelve red-shirts swinging merry at the oars and chanting a Skye *iorram*.

"Here's an exploit!" said the man of my story. "There's dignity in yon craft, or less than red-shirts was the wearing of the scamps who row her."

The loch curled like a feather before her and frothed far behind, and soon her nose ran high on the sand. No word was said, but the first pair of rowers let out a carved plank, and the fellow of my story went over it and behind to the chair with the cushioned seat.

"To the castle?" asked the captain (as it might be), in the way of one who speaks a master, and Adventurer said, "Castle be it."

The barge was pushed off the sand, the oars fell on the water, and she curved into the river-mouth.

When Adventurer reached the bridge, it was before the time of war, and the country from end to end sat quiet, free, and honest. Our folks lived the clean out-by life of shepherds and early risers. Round these hills, the woods – the big green woods – were trembling with bird and beast, and the two glens were crowded with warm homes – every door open, and the cattle untethered on the hill. Summer found the folks like ourselves here, far up on sappy levels among the hills, but their sheilings more their own than ours are, with never a reiver nor a broken clan in all the land. Good stout roads and dry went down the passes to Castle Dark from all airts of

Albainn – roads for knight and horse, but free and safe for the gentlest girl ever so lonely. By sea came gabberts of far France with wine and drink; by land the carriers brought rich cloths, spices, and Italian swords such as never were before or since. I made a small *piobaireachd* once on such a blade; if you put me over my pipes, I –

"Later the pipes, Paruig Dall, the best player in the world! to thy story this time."

Is the cup to my right or left? Blessings! The Castle and Barge were my story.

Up and on, then, under the bridge, went Adventurer and his company of twelve, and he trailed white fingers over the low side of the boat, the tide warm like new milk. Under the long arch he held up his head and whooped gaily, like the boy he was in another dream, and Mactallamh laughed back from behind the smell of lime-drop and *crotal* hanging to the stones. Then into the sun again, on the wide flat river, with the fields sloping down on each hand, nodding to the lip with rush and flower.

"Faith and here's fortune!" said Adventurer. "Such a day for sailing and sights was never before."

And the Blue Barge met nor stone nor stay, but ever the twelve fine lads swinging cheerily at the oars, till they came to the white stairs.

Off the boat and up the clanging steps went Adventurer as bold as Eachan, and the bushes waving soft on every side. The gravel crunched to his foot – the white round gravel of Cantyre; kennelled hounds cried warning from the ditch-side; round him were the scenting flowers and the feeling of the little roads winding so without end all about the garden.

"Queer is this!" said he, feeling the grass-edge with his feet and fingering the leaves. "Here, surely, is weed nor nettle, but the trim bush and the swinging rose. The gardeners have been busy in the gardens of old ancient Castle Dark!"

When he came to the ditch, the drawbrig was down. To the warm airs of the day the windows, high and low, were open; a look of throng life was over the house, and in-by some one plucked angrily at the strings of a harp. Reek rose lazy and blue over the chimneys, the smell of roasting meats and rich broths hung on the air.

Under a tree got Adventurer and deep in thought. And soon the harping came to an end. A girl stepped to the bridge and over into the garden. She took to the left by the butter-house and into My Lady's Canter, lined with foreign trees. Along the wide far road came a man to meet her, good-shaped, in fine clothes, tartan trews fitting close on leg and haunch, and a leather jacket held at the middle by a *crioslach*.

Under his tree stood Adventurer as they passed back, and close beside him the courtier pushed the hilt of a small-sword to his back and took the woman in his arms.

"Then if ye must ken," said he, shamefacedly, "I am for the road to-morrow."

The girl – ripe and full, not over-tall, well balanced, her hair waved back from over brown eyes, gathered in a knot and breaking to a curl on the nape of the neck like a wave on the shell-white shore – got hot at the skin, and a foot drummed the gravel in an ill temper.

"For yon silly cause again?" she asked, her lips thinning over her teeth.

"For the old cause," said he; "my father's, my dead brothers', my clan's, ours for a hundred years. Do not lightly the cause, my dear; it may be your children's yet."

"You never go with my will," quo' the girl again. "Here am I, far from a household of cheery sisters, so lonely, so lonely! Oh! Morag and Aoirig, and the young ones! were I back among them from this brave tomb!"

"Tomb, sweet!"

"Tomb said I, and tomb is it!" cried the woman, in a storm. "Who is here to sing with me and comfort me in the misty mornings, to hearten me when you are at wood or hill? The dreary woods, the dreary, dreary shore – they give me the gloom! My God, what a grey day!"

(And yet, by my troth, 'twas a sunny day by the feel of it, and the birds were chirming on every tree!)

The gentleman put his hands on the girl's shoulder and looked deep in her eyes, thinking hard for a wee, and biting at his low lip in a nervous way.

"At night," said he, "I speak to you of chase and the country-side's gossip. We have sometimes neighbours in our house as now, – old Askaig's goodwife and the Nun from Inishail – a good woman and pious."

Up went the lady's head, and she laughed bitter and long.

"My good husband," she said, in a weary way, "you are like all that wear trews; you have never trained your tracking but to woodcraft, or else you had found the wild-kit in a woman's heart."

"There's my love, girl, and I think you love – "

"Tuts man! I talked not of that. Love is – love, while it lasts, and ye brag of Askaig's wife and the Nun (good Lord!), and the old harridans your cousins from Lochow!"

"'Tis but a tirrivie of yours, my dear," said the man kindly, kissing her on the teeth, and she with her hands behind her back. "To-morrow the saddle, Sir Claymore and the south country! Hark ye, sweet, I'll fetch back the most darling thing woman ever dreamt of."

"What might his name be?" asked the girl, laughing, but still with a bitterness, and the two went round to the ditch-brig and in-by.

Adventurer heard the little fine airs coming from the west, coiling, full of sap-smell, crooning in turret and among the grassy gable-tops, and piping into the empty windows.

'Twas a summer's end when he went on the next jaunt, a hot night and hung with dripping stars. The loch crawled in from a black waste of sorrow and strange hills, and swished on the shore, trailing among the wreck with the hiss of fingers through ribbons of silk. My dears, my dears! the gloom of hidden seas in night and lonely places! 'Tis that dauntens me. I will be standing sometimes at the night's down-fall over above the bay, and hearkening to the grinding of the salt wash on rock and gravel, and never a sound of hope or merriment in all that weary song. You that have seeing may ken the meaning of it; never for Paruig Dall but wonder and the heavy heart!

"'Tis our thought a thousand times, just man; we are the stour that wind and water make the clod of! You spoke of a second jaunt?"

As ye say. It was in winter; and the morning –

"Winter, said ye, Paruig Dall? 'Twas summer and night before."

Winter I said, and winter it was, before *faoilteach*, and the edge of the morning. The fellow of my *sgeul*, more than a twelvemonth older, went to the breast wall and cried on Barge Blue that's ever waiting for the sailor who's for sailing on fairy seas. In she came, with her twelve red-shirts tugging bravely at the oars, and the nose of her ripping the salt breeze. Out, too, the carved plank, made, I'll warrant, by the Norwegian fellow who fashioned the Black Bed of MacArtair, and over it to the cushioned seat Adventurer!

The little waves blobbed and bubbled at the boat's shoulders; she put under the arch and up the cold river to the white stairs.

It was the middle and bloodiest time of all our wars. The glens behind were harried, and their cattle were bellowing in strange fields. Widows grat on the brae-sides and starved with their bairns for the bere and oat that were burned. But Adventurer found a castle full of company, the rich scum of water-side lairds and Lowland gentry, dicing and drinking in the best hall of Castle Dark. Their lands were black, their homes levelled, or their way out of the country – if they were Lowland – was barred by jealous clans. So there they were, drinking the reddest and eating the fattest – a wanton crew, among them George Mor, namely for women and wine and gentlemanly sword-play.

They had been at the cartes after supper. Wine lay on the table in rings and rivers. The curtains were across the window, and the candles guttered in the sconces. Debauched airs flaffed abroad in the room. At the head of the board, with her hair falling out of the knot, the lady of the house dovered in her chair, her head against George Mor's shoulder, and him sleeping fast with his chin on his vest. Two company girls from the house in the forest slept forward on the table, their heads on the thick of their arms, and on either hand of them the lairds and foreigners. Of the company but two were awake, playing at *bord-dubh*, small eyed, oozing with drink. But they slept by-and-by like the lave, and sleep had a hold of Castle Dark through and through.

Adventurer heard the cock crow away at the gean-tree park.

One of the girls, stirring in her sleep, touched a glass with her elbow, and it fell on its side, the dark wine splashing over the table, crawling to the edge, thudding in heavy drops on the shoe of the mistress of the house, who drew back her foot without waking. But her moving started up the man at her ear. He looked at her face, kissed her on the hair, and got to his feet with no noise. A sour smile curdled his face when he looked about the room, drunken and yellow-sick in the guttering candlelight.

Stretching himself, he made for the window and pulled back the curtain.

The mountain looked in on the wastrel company, with a black and blaming scowl – the mountain set in blackness at the foot, but its brow touching the first of a cold day. Tree and bush stood like wraiths all about the garden, the river cried high and snell. George Mor turned and looked at the room and its sleeping company like corpses propped in chairs, in the light of candle and daybreak.

The smell of the drunken chamber fogged at the back of his throat. He laughed in a kind of bitter way, the lace shaking at his neck and wristbands: then his humour changed, and he rued the night and his merry life.

"I wish I was yont this cursed country," said he to himself, shivering with cold. "'Tis these folk lead me a pretty spring, and had George Mor better luck of his company he was a decent man. And yet – and yet – who's George Mor to be better than his neighbours? As grow the fir-trees, some of them crooked and some of them straight, and we are the way the winds would have us!"

He was standing in the window yet, deep in the morning's grief, running his fingers among his curls.

Without warning the door of the room opened, and a man took one step in, soft, without noise, white-faced, and expecting no less than he found, by the look in his eyes. It was the goodwife's husband, still with the mud on his shoes and the sword on his belt. He beckoned on the fellow at the window, and went before him (the company still in their sleep), making for the big door, and George Mor as he followed lifted a sword from a pin.

Close by Adventurer the two men stopped. It was on a level round of old moss, damp but springy, hid from the house by some saugh-trees.

The master of the house spoke first. Said he, "It's no great surprise; they told me at the ferry over-by that strange carry-on and George Mor were keeping up the wife's heart in Castle Dark."

"She's as honest a wife as ever – "

"Fairly, fairly, I'll allow – when the wind's in that airt. It's been a dull place this for her, and I have small skill of entertainment; but, man, I thought of her often, away in the camp!"

He was taking off his jacket as he spoke, and looking past George Mor's shoulder and in between the trees at the loch. And now the day was fairly on the country.

"A bit foolish is your wife – just a girl, I'm not denying; but true at the core."

"Young, young, as ye say, man! She'll make, maybe, all the more taking a widow woman. She'll need looks and gaiety indeed, for my poor cause is lost for good and all."

"We saved the castle for you, at any rate. But for my friends in-by and myself the flambeau was at the root o't."

"So, my hero? In another key I might be having a glass with you over such friendship, but the day spreads and here's our business before us."

"I've small stomach for this. It's a fool's quarrel."

"Thoir an aire! – Guard, George Mor!"

They fought warmly on the mossy grass, and the tinkle of the thin blades set the birds chirping in the bushes, but it could not be that that wakened my lady dovering in her chair in the room of guttering candles.

She started up in a dream, and found George Mor gone, and the mark of muddy brogues near the door fitted in with her dream. She wakened none of her drugged company, but hurried to the garden and in between the foreign trees to the summons of the playing swords.

"Stop, stop, husband!" she cried before she saw who was at the fighting; but only George Mor heard, and he half turned his head.

She was a little late. Her man, with a forefinger, was feeling the way to the scabbard, and a gout of blood was gathering at the point of his sword, when she got through the trees.

"Madame," said he, cool enough but short in the breath, and bloody a little at the mouth, "here's your gallant. He had maybe skill at diversion, but I've seen better at the small-sword. To-night my un-friends are coming back to harry Castle Dark, and I'm in little humour to stop them. Fare ye weel!"

A blash of rain threshed in Adventurer's face; the tide crept at his feet, the fall of the oars on Barge Blue sank low and travelled far off. It was the broad day. Over above the river, Castle Dark grew black, but the fellow of my story could not see it.

"And the woman, Paruig Dall? What came of the woman?"

Another peat on the fire, little one. So! *That* the fellow of my story would need another trip to see. But Barge Blue is the ferry for all, high tide or low, in the calm and in the storm.

Jus Primæ Noctis

WHERE and when what I am to tell of happened, I dare not be saying in this parish. It was somewhere south of Lorn and west of the lumpy Cowal lands; it was on the edge of the salt tide; it was between two rivers and facing the morning sun – more than that I keep thumb on. When first I came on the place after my time in France, and my father's house sent a kindly reek among the alders at the twist of the way as I rode in, it was not the welcome I thought of but the story of Short Ealasaid and the Gentleman without a name. I put my chin in the air and laughed till echo hooted at me from the hills. Strange is the working of a man's mind, that when he should be full at the heart of praise and thankfulness, light things come to his head and he's off at the giggling like a fool. Here was I, at the lintel of my own door (in a manner), after six weary years among foreign swords and hagbuts for the wherewithal to keep me in brose and recreation, with the old loch sweeshing in on the chuckie-stones and the two rivers dueting high over the flute of the birds, and the smell of green growing things setting my head swounding like the fumes of a staved Nantes cask; glad, glad to the core to be back in my own place with my own folks, and yet a light tale and a sculduddry was the only occupation of my mind!

What set me on that tack was the sight of the Gentleman's garden wall at the roadside, with the moss thick and spongy on the top of it, and the brackens coming out of coil between the dry stones.

"My Gentleman's gone," said I to myself; "a creelful of bones below the clods, with his love and fancy and all the rest of it, and here's but little change! Here's the same tide swithering at the full on his foreshore, the rain-rots spreading round the trees he planted, the sappy lea's as springy to the hoof as when he put a firm brogue on it and called all the cattle he could set eye on his own."

And then I had mind of his ploy with Short Ealasaid, and laughed a good quarter by my Paris watch while my garron cropped the grass by the way.

My father (peace with him!) it was who told me the story with just as much kept back of it as befits a man's tale told at a gossiping among women and bairns, and it was not till I was far enough from my own place and the camp-fires kept me wakened that the man's bit of it came to me.

And this was the way o't.

Once upon a day in spring my Gentleman came out to survey his land, infield and outfield, tack, lot, croft, and township. He was the son of the son of a man whose name Scotland kens, and the fat Saxon will not forget in a hurry – a stout junk with the back well set and the hose doubled a bit down on as proper a leg as ever a *skene-dhu* garnished. He was black-avised, pitted a little with the plague (and there's a clue for ye!); he had a narrow brow and a dour jaw, but the soft eye of a woman newly wedded. Whether it was because of his name and dignity, or his eye and the open jollity of his word of mouth, it were hard to tell, but he had the name of a gallant in the three parishes, and when fathers came to the fair with their lasses it was "in to foot girls! we'll take round by the back way for it; for here's What's-his-name coming."

On this day the fine lusty air from the sea tingled against my Gentleman's flesh till it turned his blood from milk to brine. He snuffed the smell of sea-wrack and whins, set back his shoulders with a jerk, and felt hale and complete, like a sea-rover with a galley for his world and the tiller of it under his oxter. On every side his eye fell on his own; on the bays biting deep into the fat sides of his hills, on moor and mountain, on the deep larch woods and the corries full of bushes and the chirrup of birds, townships, and waste spots, corney-rigs and heather, the roes prancing, and the cailzie-cock flapping laggardly over the way. The heels of him spurned the road, the heart of him swelled and sung, the sinews strained at hip, knee, and elbow, and he felt like Fin Macoul.

It is a fit of the body every proper man under the two-score has now and then. I've had it myself when the year was young and the sun clean. Once it was mine on a day at Lutzen, and to slash with Sir Claymore through buff and breast-plate was like switching dockens.

In this mood then the one I speak of came to town, and just at the edge of it, lo and behold! was a girl posting blankets in a boyne, with her coats kilted and the soap sapple hardly a thought whiter than her knees. Her back was to my Gentleman, and he was close on her before she thought of turning. He pulled his bonnet a bit down on his face to keep the sun from his eyes, and looked for a little curiously at the rich curves of her and the light in her heavy brown hair glinting as if she had been redding it with the *gruagach's*[1] golden comb. She was singing in a dainty voice, a waulking song in the poor Skye Gaelic.

"Here's a new incomer, whoever she is," said he to himself, for he took credit for knowing every limmer in his land, and none there was as tall and gracious as this one busy in the boyne. Then he joined at the end of her chorus with a hearty voice, and she turned round in a hurry of hurries.

When she saw who she had, she was out of the tub in a moment, and her toes went into hiding.

---

[1] *Sea-maiden.*

"Ho, ho!" said my Gentleman, "it's you that's the dainty one! The women of hereabouts are not given to be so coy with their kirtles. You're not of my clan, *m' eudail.*" And he put an extra cock on his bonnet and set his plaid more on his shoulder, walking up to the girl's side.

"No!" she said, sharp enough. "I'm perhaps of a breed more particular. In Macleod country the gentleman are aye at the chase on the hill when the women are washing blankets."

"So! my pretty one. Poor's their taste then, if the sluts are all of your shape."

"Sluts!" said the girl with her face flaring. "Sluts, man!"

"Your mercy, my dear! I said that ere I saw sight of the face of you. There was never a slut in your family, I'll take oath on steel."

And off came the cunning man's bonnet, for all the world as if he were fronting a French demoselle.

"My face," quo' the girl, "is as God made it; but I'm thinking the Other One was on hand at the fashioning of yours."

She began to drag the boyne by one hand towards the back end of the house, and half sorry her words were out of leash. Lucky it was that words of that nature were never hounds to worry my Gentleman's vanity, and he laughed at the sally.

"Well, troth you're the good plucked one, anyway," he said, putting his bonnet on again, "and I was a churl to say what I said. I'm – So-and-so," he added.

"I kent it," said she.

"How?" asked he.

"By your gentleman's manners," said she. "A plain man would be carrying the boyne back for me."

"But – "

"But was the poorest of Fingal's dogs," said the girl, standing up straight to put a coil of her hair behind an ear like a shell.

"What was the fault of the dog?" asked my Gentleman, with his eyes swinging between the nape of her neck and her lips.

"He was an ill-bred cur."

"In what fashion, darling?"

"In an ill fashion – "

"Sharp, sharp. You're from Skye, sure enough! Might I be asking the name of so handsome an incomer to my country?"

"Your country, sir! They give you and your clan credit for many a bit land that was never won nor kept by sword or service."

And into the house went the girl, with no more heed for him.

Down the road went my Gentleman, sore confused and with less of the swank one in his gait, but hard at cogitation.

A tacksman was the first he met.

"Who's yon up at the house by the arches?" he asked, with a grip at the tacksman's plaid.

The man pulled down his eyebrows and looked up the road. He was cautious by nature.

"Is't an answer you want, or the truth of it?"

"Answer quick, man!"

"In the house up by the arches?"

"Yes, yes, *stalacaire!*"

"Well, let me see. It'll be old Paul Rhuadh's widow."

My Gentleman glowered at the man.

"Paul Rhuadh's widow! I thought she died last Whitsunday."

"So she did, so she did! I could think of nobody else, being put about regarding a heifer of mine that – "

"Who's the girl, fool?"

"On my soul, Chief, it's not gossip but learning you want! You mean the brown-haired one with the eyes. A trifle gimp about the waist?"

"She's not a Galloway quey, I'll allow, so far as shape goes, but she's posting in a boyne, and the beat of her I never saw among blankets."

"Ay, ay! ye should be a judge. But this one's too far north for your lordship. She's a Dunvegan girl, no shore-side *sgleurachd*,[1] I'll warrant. Her name's Ealasaid, and she's here at the nursing of Bell Bheg, her kinswoman."

"Ealasaid – Ailsa. Faith, 'tis a jaunty cognomen," said my Gentleman, and he turned him and went down to the Cross, rolling the name over in his mouth.

II

As my father (peace with him!) had the story, it was the next day our Gentleman left his house again with corps of stout men at his heels. There would be his gillie-cois or haunchman, his gillie-mor to carry his sword and targe, his gillie-wet-foot to take him dry over rivers, his bladair or speaker, his piper and bard, with the running lads thereto pertaining. There he was in the middle, in hunting tartan, and steel was jingling. His haunchman's man had a withie of pigeons from the doocot as a gift for the Skye girl.

When they reached the edge of the town, one of the running lads went into the house by the arches, and said the girl was to come out, for the Chief would speak to her.

"So!" said the girl, stamping her foot on the clay. "He would put this affront on me, a stranger, that he dare not for his life put on a woman of his own clan. Pigs, pigs, pigs! I have heard of the fame of ye! Go out, lackey, and tell him to call where are men to meet him."

To my Gentleman the lad went with a red face.

[1] *Slattern.*

"Well, sirrah, what said she?" asked the Chief.

"That she was not dressed in a state to come out to see you," said the lad.

"Ay, ay, woman, woman! Here's the one who knows them, black, brown, red or yellow. They're all put about for the carving of the scabbard when a man is only heeding for the stuff the blade's made of. Give me the pigeons, and come you, bladair, to put in a word with her."

My Gentleman and his spokesman went to the door, leaving the tail on the road, and the gentleman dirled on the door with the silver butt of a Doune pistol.

The girl was snodding her hair a bit and had put a brooch of a fine pattern at her throat.

"Thig stoidh!" – Come in," she cried, and they went in. She was alone, for the sick woman was but-and-ben.

"Here's for you, child," said the bladair, putting the birds on the table.

"I have no taste for tame things," said the girl, mighty quick. "Pigeons from a doocot and the courting of a poltroon – they are the two wersh things."

"From the Chief, girl," said the bladair, cautioningly.

"No Chief of mine, old man. Our Chiefs bide at home except at battles, and send their gillies on their errands."

My Gentleman was standing a bit behind, his left hand on his hip, his right by his side with his bonnet and pistol.

"Hut-trut, lass!" he broke in, "you're too clipping of the tongue for us Arraghails. Can a gentleman not give you a brace or two of fowl without this fraca?"

"Macleod women always reared their own chickens, master, and Macleod women were aye namely for having a keen eye to hawks."

"Sharp – sharp – you're from Wester Skye, sure enough! I but wanted a kiss, sweetheart."

"Troth, I'm sorry my kinswoman's so poorly. She is old enough not to be particular, and she'll know how you folks shape your mouths for it. Leave her the pigeons if you like and I'll tell her your errand."

"The devil!" cried my Gentleman. "You laugh at me. Perhaps there's a lad in the town who has your fancy. Take care, madam, where and who ye marry, for ye might be mine in any case. Ken ye my standing between the stones of this parish? I have the rights of pit, gallows, and *Primæ Noctis?"*

"If I was in a gentleman's country, I would say I had a woman's right, and that's always to the best, and a man's reverence. But it's a far cry to the well-bred land of Clan Leod, and many's the tribe between."

Right and round about turned my Gentleman, and home in a flame, on his own hard road, below his own tossing trees, over his own ditch and drawbridge, and he drank the red claret wine till nightfall. Then he went down alone, like a plain man, with his feathers out of his bonnet and the plaid on his back. But Ealasaid, the Skye girl, paid no heed to his whistling.

The summer sped, as it does in these parts, on a plover's wing, with a tail to all airts in turn, but still and on the love of my Gentleman grew no less, and the Kerched girls beyond the wall saw little of him. He lost little chance of meeting the Skye woman at Mass or market, but a man that never failed with men found himself at foil by a lass. It is the way of the chase: a hind will run farther than a stag any day.

To be on with my tale, one day my Gentleman's fox-hunter Seumas from over the hill came to him and asked if he could have three rigs more on the little field.

"What for?" asked the big man.

"For more corn," said Seumas, who was the best fox-hunter in all Albainn.

"Yes, yes, but what for should you have more land or more corn?" said my Gentleman.

"It would be for a marriage," answered Seumas.

"Whose?"

"Well, if it must be explained, it might be a fox-hunter's marriage," said Seumas, and he laughed a bit coyly.

"Ay," said my Gentleman dryly (being a bachelor by nature). "Who's the lucky one?"

"Well, I'm not what you might say altogether sure," said the fox-hunter. "There are two sisters of the Millers, strong enough girls and willing for anything, but I'm not very caring to ask one of them because the other one would be thrawn about it. Then there's a widow over-by, and another one well up in years at Croit-a-bhile."

"Do you know the girl Ealasaid in the town?" asked my Gentleman.

"Fine that," said Seumas.

"Would she be doing, do you think?"

"She's proud enough."

"She is that, sure."

"But if I had six rigs and another cow I daresay she would have me."

"Well, they're yours if you marry her."

Seumas had his own thoughts about this curious way of putting it, but he went to the one Ealasaid he knew in the town (coming as he did from the side of Nowhere at the back of beyond), and she was Short Ealasaid, who lived in the new town end, a coarse little woman getting up in years and never a beauty at the best day she had.

He asked her one question in a round-about way (thinking of the Gentleman's gallantry), and he asked her another, to which she said, "Yes," for she was sick tired making hose for three brothers and piping mutches for her mother.

In the morning Seumas came to the Gentleman and said, "Yon's fixed; we'll be married in a fortnight."

"Could you not make it a week?" said my Gentleman eagerly.

It was not a fortnight and it was not in a week, but it was in the course of time anyway that the wedding took place in the warmth of a night at the end of summer. There was dancing and there was drinking, there was the putting round of the song and the bottle *deiseilwise*.[1] The town lay deep in the darkness, fringed by the torn tide of the bays on either side, and all the life of it was in the house, where the keburs shook with the dancing of the marriage people, and the cruisies blazed far into the morning.

Well on to bedding time Seumas was cried to the door, and a gillie from up-by told him the Chief wished his wife to be sent up.

"To-morrow," said Seumas, "to-morrow's time enough; it will perhaps be about her going to the dairy."

"No," said the messenger. "To-night is the night; it is for the old cess."

"The old cess," said Seumas.

"Ay, the old cess. It's curious to me that he should put it bye without a claim so often, and call for it on you. There's a mistake somewhere, but up must your goodwife go."

"The cess; the cess – I am his own fox-hunter; surely he will not cess me. If he must, then he can have his couple of sheep and condemn his soul!"

"But he says no," said the messenger, "the wife must go up. If you would not have him down with a corps at his back, you would make the trip in the moment, both of you. I'll warrant when he sees Short Ealasaid, he'll – "

A fist in the face put an end to the messenger's story, and he went back to his master's house.

Back into the marriage house went Seumas, and he took Ealasaid into a corner. She was a squat, ugly woman (and that's the truth), with one high shoulder and a queer slit on her upper lip, with a foot on the floor like a sea-pig's flipper, but the vanity of sixteen generations of the people she came of, and they were not slack for pride.

"What for not?" she asked in a flash when Seumas spoke in her ear. "It is the custom, goodman. And 't was he that put you in the way of wedding."

"Yes, yes, but – "

"Well, *m' eudail*, it will be a scandal in the country-side if the laird does not claim his right to kiss a bride on the first night. I would not have it against me."

The man looked at her slit lip, and was struck with the notion that it never looked so slit before.

"I would send up the two sheep, as many a better man did" he said.

"Better keep the mutton," said Short Ealasaid, and she ran ben the room with a heated face to put a plaid over her marriage gown. Seumas

[1] *Left to right; sunrise*

went with her to see her up the road with hell in his heart and a dirk in his belt, and they were out and away before the company knew that my Gentleman had claimed his night's right.

My Gentleman was in his chamber in trews and buckled shoon, clean shaven and point-device like a man I saw once in a Lyons play, gulping quaichs of the red stuff and nervous at the hands, glowering at a fire of bog-fir knots frizzling on the hearth, with his back to the half-open door of his bed-closet. A rap came at the door of the room he sat in, and a man put his head in to say a woman was waiting outside.

"Let her in," said the Gentleman, with a start to his feet and the wine glucking in his thrapple. There was a minute's waiting, and then Short Ealasaid came in with a plaid on her head.

"Whom in the devil's name have we here?" cried my Gentleman.

"Ealasaid – "

"Ay, where's Ealasaid. You're her tiring-woman, maybe?"

"Me – the – day! no; I'm all that's of her."

"You are Ealasaid! What Ealasaid in God's name?"

"Ealasaid of your own name and clan, master, but now Ealasaid – Bean – Seumas, your fox-hunter's wife."

My father (peace with him!) would here tell that the Gentleman cursed high and low, far and near, by the black stones and all the imps of Ifrinn. The woman was trembling in terror, but thought it was because he would have preferred a couple of sheep.

"We can still send the mutton up," she put in.

And then my Gentleman, who, when it came to the bit, had some of the Cavalier in him, as was in all his race, behoove to spare the plain dame's feelings. In a flash he smoothed his face and laughed gaily, and turned to the woman with the Gael's welcome – and that's the open hand.

"Mistress," he said, "you have married my fox-hunter. You are the daughter of – of – "

"Iain Mor."

"Iain Mor, of course. I was wondering whether my good friend Iain could have a maid old enough to marry. Mistress, you're young, young at the business!"

It was, I'll allow, rough flattery, that would fail in many a place I've been, but it found Ealasaid on the weak spot. She reddened to the crown of her head, put a young thing's spark in her eyes, and laughed like water tinkling in a linn. "I am proud. You mind my father," said she. "We are of the Craignish folk and sib to yourself" (and there's another clue for ye), "though our lot has been poor since the Bad Year."

Then for the first time my Gentleman had a notion whom he was speaking to. She was short and slit lipped, but her father was *duineuasail*, and she had some gentility for all her thick shoon.

"Madam," said my Gentleman with a bow, putting a deep chair for her

beside the fire, "I am proud to have your father's daughter here this night."
He was thinking of a tall girl with feet in the frothy boyne and her bosom
round and generous, and here was a fat little lump!

"Wot ye what I sent for?" he asked, turning a queer fashioned silver
chain over on his fingers.

"Seumas said it was – it was – "

"Yes, mistress, it was; that same. The old cess, the *jus primæ noctis*, as
we say. To – to – kiss – "

"Yes, my lord!"

"To kiss – your hand and wish ye luck."

Ealasaid sat back stiff in her chair and her eyes looked questioning at
the man. There was a red spot on her cheek; it might be the spot a woman
has in anger, and my Gentleman was gleg enough to see it.

"And to make you this little present," he added fast, putting the chain
in her lap. (It was the chain of a powder horn; at this moment I could put
my hand on it.) "My anger when ye entered was because I had not thought
of something wiser-like for a cousin's daughter."

"My folk," said the woman a little short in the breath, "are of a high
spirit. If I thought there was a slight and that I was being lightlied – "

"Mistress, you will not think the kiss of the head of my house a slight,"
said the cunning one, watching the lines on the corner of her mouth, the
dry lips and the restlessness of her hands.

"It's not that," said Ealasaid. Then she gave a half sigh, smothered on
the way, her eyes on the round white wrist of the best man in three parishes.

"No!" cried my Gentleman in a confusion. "I was wrong to bring you
here. It was but a whim; to-morrow would have done, and I cry your
mercy."

He turned and drew back a curtain from the window to look out. The
first streak of a grey day was over Cowal Hills, and on the low horn of the
bay the cruisies were blinking in the marriage house. Over the house by the
arches the night was black and thick. A longing was at his heart, for the
lowe was gone from it and he felt a lonely man.

"I see the lights of the feast in your house," he said. "I am sorry I should
have taken you from the company and made you miss a happy hour."

"The company," said Ealasaid, "know what a Chief's right is." And she
stood to her feet, pulling her plaid tight over her shoulders, unwillingly.
She would have sat for a night on the chair for the sake of what might be
jaloused. Then she added, "Indeed, it's true, for a kiss of the hand, there
might have been no such great hurry."

It was now my Gentleman's turn to redden, and he swore soft in his
clenched teeth.

"You must drink a cup with me, goodwife, before you go," he said,
pulling the stopper from an Islay silver flask and spilling a cup of it into a

goblet.

It was done so stately, with the air of his cunning race, my Gentleman of Gentlemen, balanced on one hip with a foot out, the goblet in his white hand, and reverence in his eyes! Ealasaid gasped down the last of her hopes with a mouthful of the claret and turned to the door with a slow step.

"Good night," she said over her shoulder.

My Gentleman put out his hand eagerly, but had mind of his duty when he saw a little fire in the woman's eyes. He looked at her mouth and swithered a second, then bent humbly over her hand with his lips on her hot fingers.

"That's my right," said he.

"They have another way of it in the town's gossip," said Ealasaid, balanced on the inside foot.

"Madam," said my Gentleman, "they're aye clattering places towns. A daughter of – of – of Iain Mor and the wife of the best fox-hunter in Albainn is her own mistress in my house. I'll send some one down the road with you."

There was a noise behind my Gentleman as he spoke and the bed-closet door swung back. Out stepped Seumas with his face flaming, and him putting a dirk in its sheath.

"Your pardon, Chief; I'll see my wife down. It's as little as I could do."

"What were you doing there?" cried my Gentleman with a scowl.

"I came round by the bridge after seeing my wife in at your gate, and I found the window in-by open."

"So! You had an eye on Ealasaid had you, Seumas?"breaking into a laugh. "You would grudge me the old cess, would you?"

The woman went softly out at the door, leaving the two men facing each other.

"You missed death to-night twice by a hair-breadth," said the fox-hunter, breathing thick and fast.

My Gentleman looked under his brows at him. "How?" said he.

"If you had set a foot inside the bed-closet after my wife came to you, my dirk was in your wame."

"And the second time, my lad?"

"The second time was just before your gentleman's tongue came to you, and I thought you thought it not worth your while."

My Gentleman looked the man straight in the eyes and had a thought of the quirks of nature.

"Sir," he said at last, "I'll not deny but had I been you I'd have done it myself," and he filled another quaich of the good French wine for the fox-hunter.

A Gaelic Glossary

As compiled by Neil Munro himself

A bhean! O wife!

A pheasain! O brat!

Amadan, fool. *Amadain dhoill! O* blind fool!

Bas, the haft of a shinty in this case.

Bàs, death. *Bàs Dhiarmaid!* death to Diarmaid!

Beannachd, blessing. *Beannachd leis!* blessing with him! *Beannachd leat!* blessing with thee, farewell!

Biodag, a dirk.

Birlinn ghorm, blue barge.

Bòchdan, a ghost.

Bodach, an old man.

Bord-dubh, black-board, the game of draughts.

Bratach, a banner.

Cabar, a rafter, a log of wood for throwing in Highland sports.

Caileag bheag, a little girl.

Cailleach, old woman. *Cailleachan,* old women.

Caman, club used in the game of shinty. *Camanachd,* the game of shinty.

Cas, foot. *Cas-chrom,* a primitive hand-plough.

Choillich-dhuibh! O black-cock!

Clach-cuid-fear, a lifting-stone for testing a man's strength.

Clachneart, putting-stone.

Clarsach, harp.

Cothrom na Feinne, the fair-play of Finne; man to man.

Crioslach, belt, girdle.

Cromag, a shepherd's crook.

Crotal, lichen.

Crunluadh, a movement in piping. *Crunluadh breabach,* a smarter movement. *Crunluadh mach,* the quickest part of a piobaireachd.

Dhé! O God! *Dia,* God. *Dhia gleidh sinn!* God keep us!

Dorlach, a knapsack.

Duin'-uasal, gentleman.

Eas, waterfall or cataract.

Faoilteach, the short season of stormy days at the end of January.

Feadan, the chanter or pipe on which pipers practise tunes before playing

93

them on the bagpipes.

Fuarag, hasty-pudding, a mixture of oatmeal and cold water, or oatmeal and milk or cream.

Gruagach, a sea-maiden in this case.

'Ille! lad! *'Illean!* lads!

Iolair, eagle.

Iorram, a boat-song.

Laochain! hero! comrade!

Larach, site of a ruined building.

Londubh, blackbird.

Mallachd ort! malediction on thee!

Marag-dhubh, a black pudding, made with blood and suet.

M' eudail, my darling, my treasure.

Mhoire Mhathair, an *ave,* " Mary Mother."

Mo chridhe! my heart!

Mo thruaigh! alas, my trouble!

Och! ochan! ochanoch! ochanie! ochanorie! exclamations of sorrow, alas! *Och a Dhé! siod e nis! Eirich, eirich, Rob –* O God! yonder it is now! Rise, rise, Rob!

Oinseach, a female fool.

Piobaireachd, the symphony of bagpipe music, usually a lament, salute, or gathering.

Piob-mhor, the great Highland bagpipe.

Seangan, an ant.

Sgalag, a male farm-servant.

Sgeul, a tale, narrative.

Sgian-dubh, black knife, worn in the Highlander's stocking.

Sgireachd, parish.

Siod e! there it is!

Siubhal, allegro of the piobaireachd music.

Slochd-a-chubair gu bragh! the rallying cry of the old Inneraora burghers, "Slochd-a-chubair for ever!"

So! here! *So agad e!* here he is!

Spàgachd, club-footed, awkward at walking.

Spreidh, cattle of all sorts, a drove.

Stad! stop!

Suas e! up with it! A term of encouragement.

Taibhsear, a visionary; one with second-sight.

Tha sibh an so! you are here!

Thoir an aire! beware! look out!

Uiseag, the skylark.

Urlar, the ground-work, adagio, or simple melody of a piobaireachd.

Appendix

This short story was first published in *The Pipes of War* edited by Sir Bruce Seton (Glasgow, Maclehose, Jackson & Co., 1920). We have included it in this volume because, although written much later, it returns to the same tradition as the *Lost Pibroch* stories. It is interesting, however, that it has its setting in the First World War and illustrates Munro's ability to adapt this genre of story-telling to the harsh realities of his own time. It also compliments beautifully "The Lost Pibroch Story" itself.

THE OLDEST AIR IN THE WORLD
by Neil Munro

Col Maclean, on two sticks, and with tartan trousers on, came down between the whins to the poles where the nets were drying, and joined the Trosdale folk in the nets' shade. 'Twas the Saturday afternoon; they were frankly idling, the township people – except that the women knitted, which is a way of being indolent in the Islands – and had been listening for an hour to an heroic tale of the old sea-robber days from Patrick Macneill, the most gifted liar in the parish. A little fire of green wood burned to keep the midges off, and it was hissing like a gander.

"Take your share of the smoke and let down your weariness, darling," said one of the elder women, pushing towards the piper a herring firken. Nobody looked at his sticks nor his dragging limb – not even the children; had he not been a Gael himself Maclean might have fancied his lameness was unperceived. He bitterly knew better, but pushed his sticks behind the nets as he seated himself, and seated, with his crutches absent, he was a fellow to charm the eye of maid or sergeant-major.

"Your pipes might be a widow, she's so seldom seen or heard since you came home," said one of the fishermen.

"And that's the true word," answered Col Maclean. "A widow indeed, without her man! Never in all my life played I *piob mhor* but on my feet and they jaunty! I'll never put a breath again in sheep-skin. If they had only blinded me!"

95

There was in the company, Margaret, daughter of the bailie; she had been a toddling white-haired child when Col went to France, and had to be lifted to his knees; now she got up on them herself at a jump, an put her arms round his neck, tickling him with her fingers till he laughed.

"Oh bold one! Let Col be!" her mother commanded; "thou wilt spoil his beautiful tartan trews."

"It is Col must tell a story now," said the little one, thinking of the many he used to tell her before he became a soldier.

"It is not the time for wee folks stories," said the mother; "but maybe he will tell us something not too bloody for Sunday's eve about the Wars."

Col Maclean, for the first time, there and then, gave his tale of The Oldest Air in the World.

★ ★ ★

"I was thinking to myself," said he, "as I was coming through the whins there, that even now, in creeks of the sea like this, beside their nets adrying, there must be crofter folk in France, and they at *ceilidh* like yourselves, telling of tales and putting to each other riddles."

"*Ubh! ubh!* It is certain there are no crofters in France, whatever," said William-the-Elder. "It is wine they drink in France, as I heard tell from the time I was the height of a Lorne shoe, and who ever heard of crofters drinking wine?"

"Wherever are country people and the sea beside them to snatch a meal from, you will find the croft," insisted Col the piper. "They have the croft in France, though they have a different name for it from ours, and I'll wager the bulk of the land they labour is as bare as a bore's snout, for that is what sheep and deer have left in Europe for the small spade-farmer."

"Did'st see the crofting lands out yonder?" asked Margaret's mother.

"No," said the piper; "but plenty I saw of the men they breed there; I ate with them, and marched with them, and battled at their side, for we were not always playing the pipes, we music-fellows.

"And that puts me in mind of a thing – there is a people yonder, over in France, that play the bagpipe – they call them Brettanach – the Bretons. They are the same folk as ourselves though kind of Frenchmen too, wine drinking, dark and Papist. Race, as the old-word says, goes down to the rock, and you could tell at the first glance of a Brettanach that he was kin to us though a kilt was never on his loins, and not one word in his head of the Gaelic language. 'Tis history! Someway – some time – far back – they were sundered from us, the Brettanach, and now have their habitation far enough from Albyn of the mountains, glens and heroes. Followers of the sea, fishermen or farmers; God-fearing, good hard drinkers, in their fashion – many a time I looked at one and said to myself, 'There goes a man of Skye or Lewis!'"

"And the girls of them?" said Ranald Gorm, with a twinkle of the eyes.

"You have me there!" said Col. "I never saw woman-kind of the Brettanach; the war never went into their country, and the Bretons I saw were in regiments of the army, far enough from home like myself, in the champagne shires where they make the wine.

"We came on them first in a town called Corbie, with a church so grand and spacious a priest might bellow his head off and never be heard by the poor in the seats behind. 'Twas on a week-day, a Mass was making; that was the first and last time ever I played pipes in the House of God, and faith! that not by my own desiring. 'Twas some fancy of the priests, connived between them and the Cornal. Fifteen of us marched the flagstones of yon kirk of Corbie playing 'Fingal's Weeping.'"

"A good brave tune!" remarked the bailie.

"A brave tune, and a bonny! I'll warrant yon one made the rafters shiver! The kirk was filled with a corps of the tribe I mention – the Brettanach – and they at their Papist worshipping; like ourselves, just country folk that would sooner be at the fishing or the croft than making warfare.

"My eye fell, in particular, on a fellow that was a sergeant, most desperate like my uncle Sandy – so like I could have cried across the kirk to him 'Oh uncle! what do ye do so far from Salen?' The French, for ordinary, are black as sloes, but he was red, red, a noble head on him like a bullock, an eagle nose, and a beard cut square and gallant.

"When the kirk spilled out its folk, they hung awhile about the burial-yard as we do ourselves in Trosdale, spelling the names on the headstones, gossiping, and by-and-bye slipped out, I doubt not, to a change-house for a dram, and all the pipers with them except myself."

"God bless me!" cried Ronald Gorm.

"Believe it or not, but I hung back and sought my friend the red one. He was sitting all his lone on a slab in the strangers' portion of the grave-yard, under yews, eating bread and onion and sipping wine from his flask of war. Now the droll thing is that though I knew he had not one word of Christian Gaelic in his cheek, 'twas the Gaelic I must speak to him.

"'Just man,' says I to him. 'Health to you and a hunter's hunger! I was looking at you yonder in the kirk, and a gentleman more like my clansman Sandy Ruadh of Salen is surely not within the four brown borders of the world nor on the deeps of ocean. Your father must have come from the Western Isles, or the mother of you been wandering.'

"Of all I said to him he knew but the one word that means the same thing, as they tell me, in all Celtdom – *eaglais*. To his feet got the Frenchman, stretched out to me his bread and wine, with a half-laugh on him most desperate like Uncle Sandy, and said *eaglais* too, with a flourish of the heel of his loaf at the kirk behind him to show he understood that, anyway. We sat on the slab, the pair of us, my pipes stretched out between us, and there I assure, folk, was the hour of conversation!"

"But if you could not speak each other's tongue?" said a girl.

'*Tach!* two men of the breed with a set of pipes between them can always follow one another. 'Tis my belief if I stood his words on end and could follow them backwards they would be good Gaelic of Erin. The better half of our speech was with our hands; he had not even got the English; and most of the time we talked pipe-music, as any man can do that's fit to pucker his lips and whistle. The Breton people *canntarach* tunes too, like ourselves – soft-warbling them to fix them in the memory, and blyth that morning was our warbling; he could charm, my man, the very thrush from trees! But Herself – the *piob mhor* – was an instrument beyond his fingering; the pipes he used at home he called *biornieu*, fashioned differently from ours. Yet the same wind blows through reeds in France or Scotland, and everywhere they sing of old and simple things; you are deaf indeed if you cannot understand.

"He was from the seashore – John his name – a mariner to his trade – with a wife and seven children; himself the son of a cooper.

"I am a good hand at the talking myself, as little Margaret here will tell you, but his talk was like a stream in spate, and the arms of him went flourishing like drum-sticks. Keep mind of this – that the two of us, by now, were all alone in the kirk-yard, on a little hillock with the great big cliff of a kirk above us, and the town below all humming with the soldiers, like a byke of bees.

"He bade me play on the pipes at last and I put them in my oxter and gave him 'Lochiel's awa' to France.' A fine tune! but someway I felt I never reached him. I tried him then with bits of 'The Bugle Horn,' 'Take your gun to the Hill,' 'Bonnie Ann' and 'The Persevering Lover;' he beat time with a foot to them, and clapped my shoulder, but for all that they said to him I might as well be playing on a fiddle.

"It was only when I tried an old *port-mor* – "The Spoil of the Lowlands now graze in the Glen" that his whiskers bristled, and at that said I to myself 'I have you Uncle Sandy!'

"Before the light that flickered was gone from him I blew it up to a height again with 'Come to me Kinsman!'

"He was like a fellow that would be under spells!

"'The Good Being be about me!' cried he, and his eyes like flambeaux, 'what tune is that?'

"You never, never, never saw a man so much uplifted!

"'They call it,' said I, 'Come to me Kinsman,' (*Thigibh a so a charaid!*), and it has the name, in the small Isles of the West, of the Oldest Air of the World. The very ravens know it; what is it but the cry of men in trouble? It's older than the cairns of Icolmkill, and cried the clans from out of the Isles to Harlaw. Listen you well!' and I played it to him again – not all the MacCrimmons that ever came from Skye could play it better! for grand was the day and white with sun, and to-morrow we were marching. And many a lad of ours was dead behind us.

"When I was done, he did a droll thing then, the red fellow – put his arms about my shoulders and kissed me on the face! And the beard of him like a flaming whin!

"What must he do but learn it? Over and over again I had to whistle it to him till he had it to the very finish, and all the time the guns were going in the east.

"'If ever you were in trouble,' I said to him – though of course he could no understand me, 'and you whistled but one blast of the air, it is Col Maclean would be at your side though the world were staving in below your feet like one of your father's barrels!'"

II

The day was done in Trosdale. Beyond the rim of the sea the sun had slid to make a Sabbath morning further round the world, and all the sky in the west was streaming fire. Over the flats of Heisker the light began to wink on the Monach islets. Ebbed tide left bare sand round Kirkibost, and the sea-birds settled on them, rising at times in flocks and eddying in the air as if they were leaves and a wind had blown them. Curlews were piping bitterly.

Behind the creek where the folk were gathered on the sea-pinks, talking, Trosdale clachan sent up the reek of evening fires, and the bairns were being cried in from the fields.

The Catechist, sombre fellow, already into his Sabbath, though 'twas only Saturday nine o' the clock, came through the whins and cast about him a glance for bagpipes. he had seen Maclean's arrival with misgiving. A worthy man, and a face on him like the underside of a two-year skate-fish.

Col Maclean turned on him a visage tanned as if it had been in the cauldron with the catechu of the barking nets.

"Take you a firken too, and rest you, Catechist," said he. "You see I have not my pipes to-night, but I'm at *sgeulachd*."

But the Catechist sat not; and leaning against a net-pole sighed.

"'Twas two years after that," said Col, again into the rapture of his story, "when my regiment went to the land of wine, where we battled beside the French. I assure you we did nobly! nobly! Nor, on the soul of me! were the Frenchmen slack!"

"The French," ventured Patrick Macneill, "are renowned in story for all manly parts. Oh King! 'tis they have suffered!"

"'Tis myself, just man, that is not denying it! We were yonder in a land like Keppoch desolate after the red cock's crowing. The stars themselves, that are acquaint with grief, and have seen great tribulation in the dark of Time would sicken at the sight of it! Nothing left of the towns but *larochs* – heaps of lime and rubble where the rat made habitation, and not one chimney reeking in a hundred miles. Little we ken of trees here in the Islands, but they were yonder planted thick as bracken and cut down to the stump the way you would be cutting winter kail. And the fields that the country folk had laboured! – were the Minch drained dry, the floor of it would seem no likelier place for cropping barley or for pasturing goats.

"There was a day of days, out yonder, that we mixed up with the French and cleared the breadth of a parish of *am boche*, who was ill to shift. But the mouth of the night brought him back on us most desperate altogether, and half we had gained by noon was lost by gloaming.

"Five score and ten of our men were missing at the roll-call.

"The Cornal grunted. 'Every man of them out of Lewis!' says he; 'they're either dead or wandered. Go you out Col Maclean with your beautiful, lovely, splendid pipes, and gather at least the living,'

"Not one morsel of meat had I eaten for twenty hours, and the inside of me just one hole full of hunger, but out went Col and his pipes to herding!

"Oh King of the Elements! but that was the night most foul, with the kingdom of France a rag for wetness, and mire to the hose-tops. Rain lashed; a scouring wind whipped over the country, and it was stinking like a brock from tatters that had been men. The German guns were pelting it, the sound of them a bellow no more broken than the roar on skerries at Martinmas, the flash of them in the sky like Merry Dancers.

"I got in a while to the length of a steading with a gable standing; tuned up *piob mhor* and played the gathering. They heard me, the lads – the living of them; two-over-twenty of them came up to me by the gable, with no more kenning of what airt they were in than if a fog had found them midway on the Long Ford of Uist. I led them back to King George's furrows where our folk were, and then, *mo chreach!* when we counted them, one was missing!

"'It is not a good herd you are, Maclean,' said the Cornal, 'you will just go back and find Duncan Ban; he's the only man in the regiment I can trust to clean my boots.'

"So back went Col in search of Duncan."

"Oh lad! weren't you the gallant fellow!" cried Margaret's mother, adoring.

"I was that, I assure you! If it were not the pipes were in my arm-pit like a girl, my feet would not keep up on me the way I would be pelting any other road than the way I had to go. But my grief! I never got my man, nor no man after ever found him. I went to the very ditches where *am boche* was lying, and 't was there that a light went up that made the country round about as white-bright as the day, and I in the midst of it with my pipes in hand. They threw at me grey lead as if it had been gravel, and I fell."

"*Och, a mheudail bhochd!* – Oh Treasure!" said the women of Trosdale all together.

"I got to my knees in a bit and crawled, as it might be for a lifetime, one ache from head to heel, till I came to a hole as deep's a quarry where had been the crossing of roads, and there my soul went out of me. When I came to myself I was playing pipes and the day was on the land. The Good Being knows what I played, but who should come out across the plain to me but a Frenchman!

> "He moved as spindrift from spindrift,
> As a furious winter wind –
> So swiftly, sprucely, cheerily,
> Oh! proudly,
> Through glens and high-tops,
> And no stop made he
> Until he came
> To the city and court of Maclean,
> Maclean of the torments,
> Playing his pipes."

The Catechist writhed; the people of Trosdale shivered; Patrick Macneill wept softly, for Col Maclean, the cunning one, by the rhyming trick of the ancient sennachies, had flung them, unexpected, into the giddiness of his own swound, and all of them, wounded, dazed, saw the Frenchman come like a shadow into the world of shades.

"He flung himself in the hole beside me, did the Frenchman, gave me a sup of spirits and put soft linen to my sores, and all the time grey lead was snarling over us.

"'Make use of thy good male feet, lad,' said I to him, 'and get out of this dirty weather! Heed not the remnants of Col Maclean. What fetched thee hither?'

"He put his hand on my pipes and whistled a stave of the old tune.

"'How learned ye that?' I asked him.

"Although he was Brettanach he had a little of the English. 'Red John our sergeant, peace be with him! heard you playing it all last night,' said he, 'took a craze at the tune of you and went out to find you, but never came back. Then another man, peace be with him! a cousin of John, heard your playing and went seeking you, but he came back not either. I heard you first, myself, no more than an hour ago, and had no sooner got your tune into my head than it quickened me like drink, and here am I, kinsman!'

"'Good lad!' I cried, 'all the waters in the world will not wash out kin-ship, nor the Gael be forsaken while there is love and song.'"

"Vain tales! Vain tales!" groaned the Catechist, and hid face like a skate.

Notes and Further Glossary

Where a reference is given for a story it is *not* repeated for later stories.

Meanings of Gaelic words and phrases are in many cases already given in the Gaelic Glossary.

Abbreviations: (G) denotes Gaelic, (S) denotes Scots language

The Lost Pibroch

The Pibroch. The classical music of the great Highland bagpipe. The name comes from the Gaelic "*Piobaireachd*" meaning pipe music or pipe playing. Nowadays it is generally taken to mean *ceol mor*, big music. This intricate musical form refers to variations based on an *urlar*, a ground or theme. The variations follow in increasing complexity culminating in the *crunluath*. Pibrochs were originally taught by singing the tune to the learner player in a syllabic language called *can-ntaireached*. It is a subtle and demanding part of Highland heritage. *Ceol beag*, little music, is generally taken to be marches, strathspeys, jigs and reels.

Towsy-headed (S) With untidy hair, dishevelled, tangled.

Fingal. The warrior-god of Gaelic mythology, father of Ossian. In Gaelic his name is Fionn MacCumhail.

The Sound of Sleat. The sea-inlet between the south-east coast of Skye and the Scottish mainland. Pronounced *slate*.

The Wall of France. An old expression for the sea and particularly the English Channel.

Dirk (S) Highland dagger.

Albainn. Gaelic word for Scotland, pronounced *al-a-peen*.

Half-Town. The site of a real township on the east side of Loch Fyne and switched to the area of Inveraray by Neil Munro.

Packmen. Pedlars.

Broken men. Men without a chief to lead them who thus became fugitives.

Brogue. Shoe, from the Gaelic *brog*.

Routh. Abundance or profusion.

Sheep-fank. Sheep fold or pen.

Sheilings. The old pattern of transhumance. The Gaelic people took their herds of cows, goats and small sheep up to the higher moors and upper glens at the start of spring and returned to the lower townships at the end of summer. Temporary 'houses' of turf and stone were erected at the sheiling sites which are often in delectable spots. The beasts were fattened and butter and cheese made. The pattern was environmentally friendly and allowed the grass to grow in again at the lower townships. 'Going to the sheiling' was also a time of social pleasure – some of the most lovely Gaelic songs in praise of landscape or people, including love songs, were written at or about the sheilings. Highland games may have had their origin there with impromptu races and putting-the-stone.

Notes

Strathlachlan. An area on the east side of Loch Fyne, south of Strachur. Pronounced *Stra-loch-lin*.

Dundarave. The old MacNaughton stronghold on the north-west shore of Loch Fyne and restored by architect Sir Robert Lorimer in 1911. It is the prototype of Doom Castle in Neil Munro's novel of that name (1901). Pronounced *doon-da-rav* from the Gaelic *dun da ramh*, the fort of the two oars.

Lochow. Loch Awe.

Crouse (S) Bold, confident, courageous.

Easachosain. A waterfall in a narrow glen near Auchnabreac, south of Inveraray. Pronounced *ess-ach-awson*.

Duglas Water. Modern Douglas Water, a river south of Inveraray.

Horn Spoon. Made from cattle horn.

Port (G) Tune.

Paruig Dall (G) Blind Peter, pronounced *Pahrig Dahl*.

Bothy. A small cottage. From the Gaelic *bothan*.

Pirn (S) Spool for thread or a bobbin.

Cogie (S) Bowl, generally made of birch wood.

"Muinntir a' Ghlinne so", "People of this Glen", in Gaelic pronounced *mooincheer a ghleenyi shaw*. A pipe tune. It was played by a Campbell piper to warn the MacDonalds of Glencoe of the imminent massacre.

Siubhal (G) A movement of pibroch. Pronounced *shoo-awl*.

Shanks (S) Legs.

Oxter (S) Armpit.

Padric Og (G) Little Peter, pronounced *Pahtrick awk*.

Kintail. An area of the north-west Highlands, including Loch Duich and Lochalsh, the lands of the Clan MacRae.

Glen Coe. Site of the infamous massacre of February 13, 1692, when a detachment of a regular regiment of the British Army, under the command of Robert Campbell of Glen Lyon, killed around 30 MacIains or McDonalds of Glencoe whose chief had failed to meet the deadline to take an oath of allegiance to King William of Orange. The deed has been widely regarded as particularly evil because the laws of Highland hospitality were abused in that the soldiers, on orders from the garrison at Fort William, turned treacherously on their unsuspecting hosts.

Corri. Corrie, a hollow in the hills, from the Gaelic *coire*.

Brae (S) Hillside, a stretch of ground rising fairly steeply.

Smooring. Smouldering. House fires were smoored at night long ago by raking the ashes over the embers which could be re-activated in the morning.

Diarmaid. A Campbell. Diarmad O'Diubhne was a Celtic warrior from whom the clan derives its pedigree. Pronounced *djeeramitch*.

Dunvegan. The castle of the MacLeods on the island of Skye, famed for its hospitality. Pronounced *doon-vehgan*.

Cairn Dubh to the Creaggans. Cairn Dubh, the Black Crag, is modern Cairndow, near Ardkinglas House, on the shores of Loch Fyne. The Creggans lies several miles south of Cairndow. (G) *na creagan*, the crags.

Crusie-light. A small light composed of a wick of rushes or a fir cone set in a little wood or stone bowl. Some cruisie-lights burned seal or fish oil. The name derives from the Gaelic *cruisgean*.

Alowe (S) Alight.

Ken (S) Know.

"Thug mi pòg…". The verse translates literally as:
"I gave a kiss and a kiss and a kiss,
I gave a kiss to the king's hand,
No one who ever blew wind into a sheep's hide
Received such hospitality apart from me!"
The 'bag' of the bagpipe was made from sheepskin.

Night-hags. Owls.

Drones. A set of wooden pipes, two tenor and one bass, each producing a constant note. Part of the bagpipe.

Moideart (G) An area of the western Highlands (Moidart), north of Ardnamurchan.

Macruimen (G) The MacCrimmons were the most distinguished piping family and were always hereditary pipers to the MacLeods of Dunvegan. They had a college of piping at Boreraig, on Skye.

Bawbee (S) A small value copper coin, equivalent to six pennies Scots or one half penny sterling (1.2p).

Cockle. A shell.

Cowal. The 32-miles long peninsula which divides Loch Fyne from the Clyde Estuary. It is reputedly named from Comhgall, grandson of King Fergus of Dalriada.

Beinn Ime. The 1011m (3318ft) mountain to the east of Glen Croe, Argyll, the highest of the 'Arrochar Alps'. The name means butter mountain, a reference to a sheiling area. Pronounced *Eem-eh*.

Galley of Lorn. A galley is a boat. The area of Lorn takes its name from Lorn, son of Erc, whose kingdom it was around AD 500. It includes all the land between Loch Awe and the Firth of Lorn. Loch Leven is the northern boundary and the Bealach Mor, the Great Pass, at the head of Loch Craignish, is the southern. The galley with oars and sail appears in many heraldic designs. It was originally an ancient heraldic symbol of the Norse Kingdom of the Isles, adopted by Somerled and his descendants, notably the MacDougall Lords of Lorne and MacDonald Lords of the Isles. Later heraldry made the Galley of Lorn distinct by giving it a silver instead of gold background. It went with the Lordship of Lorne to the Stewarts and then the Campbells. Many Campbells, not just chiefs, have it in their arms.

Glen Shira. The long glen running north-east from Loch Shira, a side-loch of Loch Fyne, and which was greatly loved by Neil Munro. The name derives from the Gaelic *siorabh*, the lasting river.

Gilleasbuig Gruamach. Archibald the Grim, the 8th Earl and 1st Marquis of Argyll. Pronounced *Geel-espig Groo-amach*. He succeeded to the title in 1638 and was notorious for his cruelty and duplicity.

Boshang. The entrance to Glen Shira. When Mary Queen of Scots visited her half-sister, the 5th Countess of Argyll, she was taken on a visit to Glen Shira and is reputed to have exclaimed "Quel beau champ" which has been contracted to Boshang.

Beinn Bhuidhe. The Yellow Mountain, (948m, 3106ft), sited between the head of Glen Shira and Glen Fyne.

Carnus (G) A ruined township in Glen Aray, north of Ladyfield, the Lecknamban of Neil Munro's stories.

Ben Bhreac. A mountain near Loch Awe. The name in Gaelic means dappled or speckled mountain.

Beltane. The Celtic new year, normally celebrated around May.

Scart (S) Scraping.

Stot (S) Bullock.

Heifer. Young cow.

Milch-cow. Cow which has calved and is in milk.

Strath. (G) *srath*. A wide and open valley.

Steep we the withies. Willow branches were steeped in water to make them pliable for basket making or other tasks. It was a job to be accomplished before leaving home for any length of time.

The Honey Croft. A lodge of Inveraray Castle now stands on this site close to the police station and is known as Croitaville.

So! So! (G) Here! Here! (pronounced *Shaw, shaw*).

Craig-an-Eas. Crag-of-the-Waterfall, a common name in Argyll. Pronounced *Craik-an-ess*.

Maam-side. Maam is a farm in Glen Shira. Maam-side is the hill land of the farm.

Wersh (S) Sour.

Cruachan. Ben Cruachan (1126m, 3689ft) above Loch Awe, Argyll. This is Cruachan Beann in Gaelic, the-heaped-up-mountain. "Cruachan!" is the Clan Campbell war slogan and is pronounced *croo-achan*. The slogan derives from a gathering place called Cruachan opposite Innischonnel.

Dunchuach. The small 913ft hill above Inveraray, much loved by Neil Munro and which features in his historical novels. It had an almost fey attraction for him. In *John Splendid* (1898) he places a fort on its summit and depicts a Campbell garrison holding out in 1645 against assaults by the men of the Royal army of James Graham, Marquis of Montrose, and Alasdair MacColla, war leader of Clan Donald and Montrose's major-general. The real folly-tower on the summit which can be seen from the town was erected in 1747. The hill's name derives from *Dun na Cuaich*, Fort of the Cup. An Iron Age fort was once sited there. Most local people pronounce the name as *Dunny-quaich*, but *Dun-choo-ich* is also said. (Inveraray should be pronounced *Inver-ay-rah*). There are wide views from its summit particularly down Loch Fyne.

Blessings with thee. Traditional Gaelic farewell.

The King of Errin. A reference to an old legend. Scots and Irish Gaelic culture was often intertwined.

Black cattle. Many of the small Highland cattle long ago were coloured black. The big, shaggy 'Highlander' we see today is a 19th-century cross-breed. The colour black – plus nefarious deeds – also gave us the origin of the word blackmail ('mail' is an old Scots word for rent): the MacGregors and other clans asked Lowland lairds for protection money to stop cattle raids. Reiving (stealing) cattle was considered a manly sport, rather than a crime, long ago. In his novel *John*

Splendid Neil Munro depicts Colin of Elrigmore's father making this point to Colin.

Droves. Huge herds of cattle were once driven from the Highlands and Islands to the big fairs or trysts at Crieff, in Perthshire, or at Falkirk, Stenhousemuir, Reddingmuirhead and Rough Castle in the Central Lowlands. The trade was vibrant from the late 16th century well into the 19th century when changed transport and agricultural practices ended it. Many of the beasts went as far south as Norwich or Carlisle. The roast beef of old England frequently came from Scotland. The grassy tracks of the drovers can still be seen in the hills and Neil Munro brings them into his historical novel, *The New Road* (1914).

Glen Beag and The Rest. Gleann Beag means the Little Glen; it runs between Loch Goil and Loch Fyne. The Rest is the Rest-And-Be-Thankful viewpoint at the crest of Glen Croe, between Arrochar and Glen Kinglas. It is an old drovers' route. The 18th-century military road built to curb cattle raiding and the Jacobite clans, and the modern A83 road (linking Loch Fyne and Loch Long) both follow the same line. In his historical novel, *The New Road*, Neil Munro depicts his hero, Aeneas MacMaster, travelling north on horseback on this route until he joins up with the scout-agent, Ninian MacGregor Campbell, at Bridge of Orchy, north of Tyndrum.

The Red Hand

Iain Mor. Big John.

Drimfearn (G) A farm in Glen Aray, "the ridge of the alders".

Kilmune (G) A farm in Glen Aray, named after chapel of the Celtic St. Mun.

Salachary (G) A farm in Glen Aray, "the sheiling of the willows".

"Bodaich nam Briogais". There are some anachronisms in this story. "*It was... before the wars that scorched the glens; and Clan*

Campbell could cock its bonnet in the face of all Albainn..." This would imply before the 17th century. Black Duncan is said to be Chief of the Campbells. The last Campbell Chief of this name was the Sir Duncan Campbell (The Black Knight of Lorne) who was chief from around 1414 to 1453. There were later chieftains of the Campbells of Glenorchy by the name Duncan but the repeated use of the title

"Lochow" shows that the Chief in the story was the Campbell Chief himself (Black Duncan of the Castles is equally anachronistic). But the Piper is playing such tunes as *"Bodaich nam Briogais"* ("The Old Men Wearing The Breeks") which is said to have been composed in 1680 at the battle of Allt nam Mearlach, near Wick, in Caithness, when Glenorchy and his Highlanders defeated the trews-clad Sinclairs. "I got a Kiss o' the King's Hand" is supposed to have been composed by the MacCrimmon of the day, acknowledged as the leading piper who was so honoured by King Charles II before the Battle of Worcester in 1651.

Black Duncan's Tail. The chief's personal retinue.

Tearlach (G) Charles or Charlie, pronounced *Charlach.*

Giorsal (G) Grace.

Boar's Head. Diarmad, the progenitor of Clan Campbell, is reputed to have killed a wild boar.

Lecknamban. In Glen Aray, "the slope of the women", hence Ladyfield. (G) *Leac nam ban.*

Tearlach Og. Young Charles.

Duniveg's Warning. This tune is better known as *The Piper's Warning to his Master* and refers to an incident when a trap was laid for Colkitto MacDonald at his castle of Duniveg on Isla. His piper played this tune to warn him that the castle was occupied by his enemy. In revenge the piper was horribly put to death.

The black bitch from Dunstaffnage. Janet Campbell – also known as "the most beautiful woman in Argyll" – was the daughter of Campbell of Dunstaffnage, and wife of George Campbell of Airds. Her involvement with Colkitto is another legend which has become confused with the Duniveg incident.

Feather. The use of an eagle feather to denote rank may be a 19th-century invention.

The Dogs of Lorn. Mythical dogs of the MacDougalls.

Alaistair Corrag. (G) *corrag* means forefinger.

Black Bull slope. A slope at the foot of Glen Aray. (G) *tarbh dubh.*

Carloonan. On the banks of the Aray half a mile beyond the castle. The old spelling was Carlundan. It probably derives from (G) *car*, the winding or meandering of a stream, and *lunndan*, a green meadow or marshy ground.

Cladich. Near the head of Loch Awe. The ancestral home of the MacIntyres who were famous for knitted garters.

Three Bridges. In Glen Aray, three miles north of Inveraray.

The Secret of the Heather-Ale

Clan Artair. The MacArthurs of Lochaweside (there are several other unrelated septs of the same name) are possibly an early offshoot of the same stock as the Campbell chiefs. They appear to have been a learned family whose Charles MacArthur was the "doer" or man of business to the Earl of Argyll. He was rewarded c.1510 with the grant of the lands of Tiravadich. From then on, the advance of the family around the head of Loch Awe was swift, causing much annoyance with the neighbouring Campbells of Inverawe. In 1547, the "Chief of Clan Arthur" was drowned with the "Chief of Clan Viccar" in a skirmish with the Inverawe Campbells in Loch Awe.

Antrim and his dirty Irishmen. The Earl of Antrim was a member of Clan Donald South, the MacDonalds of Islay, descended from John Mor, younger brother of the Lord of the Isles, whose 14th-century marriage to the Bisset heiress of the Glens of Antrim brought much land in Ulster to the family. A member of this family, Randal MacDonnell, was created Earl of Antrim in 1620. A cousin of the Earl was *Coll Ciotach* MacDonald – Coll the left-handed – who held the Island of Colonsay. His son was Alasdair MacColla, appointed by Antrim to lead the strong contingent of Clan Donald who joined the Royalists in a glorious 17th-century attempt to revenge themselves on their sworn enemies, the Campbells. Alasdair was appointed Major-General by the King's Lieutenant, Montrose, and in his invasions of Argyll behaved with the utmost ferocity against his clan's old foes.

Flambeaux. Torches.

Baracaldine. In Benderloch. One of the seven castles built by Duncan Campbell of Glenorchy. The Campbells of Barcaldine descended from Para, an illegitimate son of Campbell of Barcaldine. They were for several generations factors for their cousins, the Campbells of Glenorchy (later Earls of Breadalbane) on their extensive lands in Argyll.

Niall Mor a' Chamais. Big Neil of Kames. He may not have been a real person. The fact that he is mentioned as appearing in "the writings of Lord Archie" (Lord Archibald Campbell, brother of the 9th Duke and father of the 10th, a prolific author on local matters), may be a humorous claim to his historical existence.

Hose. At this period "stockings" were cut out of tartan material (often in *cath dath* – red and white dice), shaped to the leg and held up by garters; later replaced by better fitting knitted stockings.

Tullich. A round, flat hill in Glen Aray.

"Baile Inneraora". "The Town of Inveraray". Early title of the tune now better known as "The Campbells are Coming", the march of Clan Campbell.

Altan Aluinn (G) A burn in Glen Shira, the name of which is "beautiful streamlet".

The Foal's Gap. Part of the River Aray above the bridge which crosses above Carloonan. Munro talks of it being past Maam which is in Glen Shira. He sometimes moved sites around.

Mackellars. An old Argyllshire sept whose chief family appears to have been Mackellar of Ardary.

Stot (S) Bounce.

Kittle (S) Poke.

Gall (S) Bog myrtle.

Calum Dubh. Black Malcolm.

Elerigmor (G) From *eileirg* meaning a pen wider at one end than the other used to trap deer. Elrigmore and Elrigbeg are farms in Glen Shira. Colin of Elrigmore is one of the two main heroes in the novel *John Splendid.*

Basket-hilt A guard for the hand on a sword, so-called because it looked like basket work.

Tom-a-Phubaill. A hill in the upper part of Glen Shira near the Shira dam and which means the hill of the butter-bur.

Ferrara sword. Swords reputedly made by Andrea Ferrara, the 16th-century Venetian sword maker, were greatly prized in the Highlands for balance and strength.

Target or targe. A round Highland shield.

Sgian Dubh. A black knife, so-called because it was often made from coarse metal.

Yon (S) That.

Dour (S) Grim.

Smirr (S) Brushing, light covering.

Herd. Cowherd, drover.

Art. Probably cognate with Artair, Arthur.

Uileam. William.

Drimlea (G) A farm in Glen Shira, "the grey-ridge".

Blaranbuie (G) "The little yellow glade". A wooded hillside above the Dubh Loch in Glen Shira.

Ploy. Project.

Yont (S) Yonder.

Tow (S) Rope.

Scaurnoch. This name is used where there is a scree or continuous run of stones on a hillside. There is a place above the Dubh Loch of that name, but in the context it is almost certainly the rockface on Dunchuach.

Kilblaan. A farm in Glen Shira, named after a chapel of St Blaan.

Ardno. A hill across Loch Fyne, north of Ardkinglas House.

French Foreland. A headland between Inveraray and Furnace on the shores of Loch Fyne. The French boats would land to barter their wines for herring.

Hell's Glen. Gleann Beag between Lochgoilhead and Loch Fyne. It may get its nickname from the difficulty of passage in winter.

Sithean Sluaidhe (G) "The hill of the fairy people". Probably refers to the fairy hill on Cruach nan Capull opposite Furnace.

Scart (G) *scarbh*. The cormorant or shag.

Boboon's Children

Knapdale. The area north west of Kintyre. The name derives from the Norse for a rounded but prominent point of land, *knapp*, and *dalr*, river valley.

Swart. Sun-burned. Proud or jaunty is also appropriate.

Wade's Roads. The 18th-century military roads constructed to tame the Jacobite clans and to stop cattle reiving (raiding) and named after Field Marshal George Wade (1673-1748), Commander-in-Chief in Scotland in 1724 with the task of demilitarising the Highlands. The theme of the military roads and their effects on trade and Gaelic culture dominates the plot of Neil Munro's historical novel, *The New Road* (1914).

Fingalian Tales. Legends and stories from Celtic mythology linked to the warrior Fingal or Fionn.

Lures. Fishing flies.

Iain Og of Isla. John Campbell of Islay (1821–85), a grandson of Lady Charlotte Campbell and Walter Campbell of Shawfield. Lady Charlotte was the daughter of the 5th Duke of Argyll. Known as Iain Og Ile (Young John of Islay), he was a collector of local tales and traditions and the writer of *Popular Tales of the West Highlands*.

Braevallach. The brae or slope of the pass on the east side of Loch Awe.

Clapped. Quickly thrust.

Pickle (S) A little or small amount.

Collogue (S) Talk, mingle, share.

The wall of old Quinten. Quinten Wright was Provost (the equivalent of English mayor) of Inveraray and lived in the house which is now the Bank of Scotland in Church Square. In the garden of this house a monument was erected to 17

Campbell leaders who were executed on that spot by men from Atholl. Neil Munro's reference in the story is to another conflict, the Battle of Inverlochy in 1645 during the Scottish Wars of the Covenant, when a Convenant army – mainly composed of Campbells – was overwhelmingly defeated by the Royalist army of the Marquis of Montrose. The stone's inscription is in Latin. In recent years it was considered unsafe and moved to a site near Inveraray Castle. The wall between the end of the bank and the tenement know as Relief Land is known as Boboon's Wall. The garden side of the wall is much higher than the street side and that is why Boboon could easily lean over the wall and talk to his tribe.

The Blue Quarry. A quarry behind Inveraray on the outside of the Great Beech Avenue. Flagstones were quarried here and the rubble used in some of the town buildings.

Conan's Curse. There is a well at Dalmally dedicated to the Celtic Saint Conan.

Beannan. A croft in the old town common land. It is no longer visible, but the name is perpetuated in a large boulder, an erratic from the Ice Age which sits on the hillside near the farm of Balantyre, in Glen Aray. The name means a pinnacle.

"Failte an Roich". "Munro's Welcome".

Stravaig (S) To wander or to roam.

Plotted (S) Boiled.

Tunnag (G) Duck.

Collop. Slice, portion.

Gralloch. Disembowel, gut.

Moor Rannoch. A great stretch of bog, heather and ancient forest between Glencoe and Rannoch-side. Modern

Rannoch Moor. The moor was once home to the bear, elk, wolf, beaver and other animals now extinct in Scotland and was refuge for fugitives or 'broken men'.

Stuc Scardan (G) A hill which stretches from Glen Shira to a ridge overlooking Glen Aray. *Stuc* means a sharp-pointed hill and *scardan*, a screeface (area of continuous small stones).

Thrawed (S) Wrung.

Stron. The point opposite Inveraray, known as Strone Point, from (G) *sron*, a nose.

Gabbert (S) Sailing boat.

Dyke. A drystane wall.

Shelister. (G) *seilisdeir*, the wild yellow iris.

Donnacha Ban's, *"Coire Cheathaich"*. A popular song/poem, "The Misty Corrie", by the Gaelic poet, Duncan Ban Macintyre (Donnachadh Ban Nan Oran, Fair Duncan of the Songs), 1724–1812. The lines quoted are based only loosely on the original poem (cf. *l.*2357ff.).

Stoury (S) Dusty.

Bide (S) Stay.

Causey. Paved road.

Kilmichael Market. Cattle drovers from the islands of Islay and Jura and from Kintyre met at Kilmichael, in mid-Argyll, to sell cattle or to rest en route to the great trysts at Falkirk.

Saugh-wand (S) Willow branch.

Thong. As thin as a leather lace or thong.

Macvicar's Land. A small tenement in the town of Inveraray between Arkland and the avenue wall: a family called MacVicar once lived there, as did Neil Munro.

Ridir (G) Knight.

Snodding and redding. Tidying up, making neat.

Bossy. Green, verdant.

Cantrips (S) Impish revels or pranks.

Coillevraid. A croft in the town common land. The name means "wood on the braeface".

Brochan (G) Porridge.

Garron. The short river which empties from the Dubh Loch into Loch Shira.

The factor's corner. The chamberlain or factor's house was built on the corner of Main Street and Front Street and next to what was the Town House, but is now the tourist office.

Bas (G) The haft of a *caman* or shinty stick. Shinty is a cousin of Lacrosse, the Irish hurley and modern hockey and is a full-blooded and manly game.

Cas (G) Foot.

The Arches. The screen Arch in Inveraray extending from the Great Inn across the Dalmally road. It was built in the 18th century as part of the New Town.

Winterton. A field in front of the castle where cattle were enclosed and fed in winter.

Kennachregan. A hill in Glen Aray backing on to Glen Shira.

The Fell Sergeant

Gug-gug. Cuckoo sound.

Tom-an-dearc (G) The hillock of the berry.

Daunder (S) Saunter.

Caird. (G) *ceard*, tinker.

Bana-Mhuileach. A wife or woman from Mull.

Swear't. Reluctant (sweart).

"Mo Nighean Dubh". "My Black-haired Maiden".

Aoirig (G) Euphemia or Effie.

Throng (S) Busy.

Press. Wall cupboard.

Duart. An eastern area of the island of Mull which contains the MacLean's stronghold, Castle Duart.

Inishail. An island in Loch Awe which contains an ancient burial ground.

Kilmalieu. The burial ground at Inveraray, on the shores of Loch Fyne.

Glenurchy. The old spelling of modern Glen Orchy which links Loch Awe-side with Achallader and the road to Glencoe.

Haver (S) A wandering of the mind.

Wright. Carpenter or joiner.

Badenoch. From the Gaelic *Baideanach*, the 'drowned land': the Highland area north of Atholl and east of Lochaber and mainly the land of Clan Chattan, a federation of clans, particularly the MacKintoshes.

Ditty. A verse or part of a song.

Thrawn (S) Obstinate, 'cussed'.

Cousin-german. First (or at any rate very close) cousin.

Preeing (S) Tasting, sampling.

Quaich. (G) *cuach*, drinking cup.

Niall Ban. Fair Neil.

Agus ho-e-ro! Gaelic for 'and' and then a phonetic chorus like fal-de-ral.

Mor (G) Great or big.

Ben the house. Inside the house.

Goodwife. A polite form of address for the mistress of a house.

Gluck (S) Gurgle.

Sneck (S) Latch.

Black Murdo

Mas breug uam e is breug thugam e. Gaelic proverb, "If it's a lie from me it is a lie to me": i.e. passing on something the teller is not entirely sure of.

Stronbuie. Yellow promontory from (G) *sron*, nose, and *buidhe*, yellow.

Red Duke. The 2nd Duke of Argyll. A famous soldier, who fought in the wars of the Spanish Succession and commanded the Hanoverian army at the battle of Sheriffmuir in 1715. He was known to Gaels as Red John of the Battles.

Fraoch Eilean... Innis Chonain. Islands on Loch Awe (heather island and island of St. Conan).

Innis Chonnel. The island on Loch Awe where the Campbells had their original stronghold before moving to Inveraray in the 15th century.

Inishail. The holy island of Loch Awe and once a base for Cistercian nuns. It was the burial ground of the district.

Innistrynich. This name derives from Innis Draighnich, isle of the blackthorn shrubbery. Situated at the north end of Loch Awe, it was originally owned by the MacArthurs and once housed a small monastery linked to the nunnery on Inishail. It is a promontory, not an island.

Skilly woman (S) Midwife.

Atholl dogs. The Jacobite clans from Atholl who sometimes raided Argyll.

Corranach (G) Lament.

Recked. Reckoned, judged.

Silis. Gaelic name, popularly associated with Julia.

March-dyke (S) Boundary wall.

Portinsherrich (G) *Port-innis-sia-ramhach*, the

port of the island of the six-oared galley. Sited halfway down the east side of Loch Awe.

Clan Alpin. The MacGregors.

Ell. A length measure, generally for cloth.

The brand of a cross on her brow. Branded as identification as a witch.

The Glenurchy Woman. A noted Highland witch.

The black stones. Stones with reputed supernatural powers were sometimes used for healing processes.

Strong Colin. Possibly a warder for Clan Diarmad at Inveraray.

Dunt (S) Thud.

Alt Shelechan. (G) *allt seileachan*, "the burn of the willows" in Glen Aray.

Crousely (S) Confidently.

Sweelers (S) Swaddling clothes for a baby.

Toll. Payment for passage.

Flaff. A flutter.

Gow an Aora. Glen Aray has the ruins of a settlement called Ballygowan, the smith's steading. Gow an Aora translates as "The Smith of Glen Aray".

Bucklers. Shields or targes.

Dirl (S) Vibrate.

Kyloes. Highland cattle.

Blithe-meat. Food taken to celebrate the birth of a child.

"Wheesht". "Hush".

II

The Spotted Death. The plague.

Warm-happed (S) Warmly wrapped.

Brosey. The common people, who ate oatmeal brose.

The Holy Iron. Oaths were sworn on the

blade of a dirk. Iron was hostile to fairies and fended off supernatural harm.

The Lamonts got their bellyful. The Campbells executed Lamont leaders after they supported Montrose and Alasdair MacColla in the 17th-century Scottish Wars of the Covenant.

The Stewarts took their best from Appin. Inveraray was plundered by Montrose's men who had Stewart contingents in the Royal army.

Slochd-a-chubair. The Cooper's Pool where

the river Aray enters Loch Fyne.

Rowth (S) Plentiful.

Sennachie. (G) *seanachaidh*, a story teller.

Crowdie (S) Soft cheese.

Ard Rannoch. Fern Point, the promontory of land on which was built the New Town of Inveraray in the 18th century.

Wrack. Seaweed.

Reek (S) Smoke.

Malison. Curse.

Bock (S) Retch.

The Sea-Fairy of French Foreland

Grat (S) Sobbed.

Gowsty (S) Blustery, eerie.

Seven. This number was regarded as having 'special' or supernatural significance.

Salmon. This fish had mystic qualities and was reputed to have eaten the Hazel Nuts of Knowledge. The Dukes of Argyll wear salmon shaped buttons on Highland dress.

Gleg (S) Quick.

Loch Steallaire-bhan. A man-made water supply loch above Inveraray. The name means a white cascade.

Gruagach (G) A female spectre of the class of brownies or sea maidens. She presided over cattle and milkmaids made libations to her.

Thrapple (S) Throat.

Ceannmor Modern Kenmore, the big headland. A Loch Fyne village built by the Duke of Argyll for crofters/fishermen.

French traffickers. There was a thriving trade between French traders and Inveraray fishermen long ago, commemorated in the name French Foreland.

Dalchenna. Kenneth's Field, a farm south of Inveraray.

Black-avised. Black-haired and dark of countenance.

Forbye (S) As well.

Behooved (S) Felt it wise.

Marseli (G) Often spelled Marsailidh. Equivalent of Marjorie.

Meal. Oatmeal.

Tailor-tartans. Tiny sea-creatures found under stones on the shore.

Spout-fish. Razor fish, a type of shellfish found in sand.

Lobbies. Hallways.

Charlie Munn. The lands of Clonary in the story belonged to the McPhuns.

Crack (S) Chat.

Beann Francie. The wife of Frank. (G) *bean*, wife.

The Horse Pack. A small cottage on the main road above Dalchenna.

By-ordinar (S) Unusually.

Sea-pig. (G) *muc mara*, whale.

Tarbert. The port on East Loch Tarbert and close to West Loch Tarbert which separates south Knapdale from the Kintyre peninsula.

Douce (S) Sedate, comfortable.

Cromalt. Cromalt is a burn south of Inveraray and this name was given by Neil Munro to his house in Helensbugh.

Dud (S) Rag.

Chuckie stones (S) Small pebbles, generally white.

Breckan (S) Bracken.

111

Shudderman Soldier

Catechist. A person who instructed others in Christian doctrine.

Dhuloch-side. Beside Dubh Loch at the foot of Glen Shira.

The cock of the mountain. The blackcock.

White grouse. The ptarmigan.

Tryst. A meeting.

Quey's Rock. A rock on Balantyre Hill in Glen Aray. Quey (S) is a heifer.

Posting (S) Tramping in the washtub.

Ellar Ban. Fair Ellar.

Clan Coll. The MacDonalds.

A boll of meal. A dry measure or weight of oat-meal.

Donacha. Duncan.

Brattie (S) Pinafore.

Arthur's children. Clan Arthur.

Canny (S) 'Of good omen'.

Dol' (G) Phonetic spelling of *Domhnall*, Donald.

Francie Ro. Local name for Francis Munro. Neil Munro was known in Inveraray as Neilly Ro.

Peching (S) Panting.

Dourly (S) Grimly.

Fencibles (S) Army units raised for home ser-vice only.

Poke (S) Bundle or bag.

Wean (S) Child.

Shauchling (S) Shuffling, shambling.

Clout (S) A cloth.

Dipping-time. The time for dipping sheep against parasites.

Snedding (S) Trimming.

Stronmagachan. A farm in Glen Aray, the name of which perhaps means frog point.

Jagging. Prickling.

Chief enough with (S) Close enough to.

Braxy (S) Mutton from a sheep that had died of the disease.

Farl. A small piece.

Taravhdubh (G) The Black Bull. The name of a slope at the foot of Glen Aray.

Blear. Shining dimly.

Dressing her son's corpse. Preparing the corpse for burial.

War

Quirky (S) Twisting.

Closes (S) Passageways between the houses and leading inside to different levels.

MacCailein Mor. The Gaelic title for the Duke of Argyll. Literally "Son of Great Colin" (the 13th-century Sir Colin Campbell of Loch Awe).

Culross girdle. The Fife town was once famous for making iron girdles. Culross is pronounced *coo-ross*.

Bannock (S) Bread-scone.

Scad (S) Glow.

Crarae. On Loch Fyne-side, between Furnace and Minard.

Bide it (S) Stand it, bear it.

Inverlochy dogs. A reference to the victors at the great Campbell defeat at Inverlochy, near Fort William, in 1645 during the Scottish Wars of the Covenant.

Tearlach (G) Charles, Prince Charles Edward Stuart, who raised his standard

at Glenfinnan in 1745 against the Hanoverian government but was defeat-ed at Culloden in 1746.

Duddy (S) Ragged, tattered.

"Bundle and Go". Pipe tune now known as "The Campbells are Coming".

Cantyre. The old spelling of Kintyre.

The march of Keppochan. The parish bound-ary between Glen Aray and Inishail.

Played dirl (S) Vibrated.

Rig. Cultivation terrace.

Elrigmor. A farm in Glen Shira. In this case it refers to the owner of the farm.

Geordies. Nickname for coins with the heads of George I and II on them.

Lifting (S) Reiving or stealing cattle.

Cooper's Pool. Where the River Aray enters Loch Fyne.

Ganting (S) Yawning.

Glee'd. Ready for firing. A reference to the cannon known as the 'Glede Gun' now at

Inveraray Castle. From (S) *glede*, spark.

Kilmarnock bonnet. A broad flat woollen bonnet manufactured in Kilmarnock in Ayrshire.

Land (S) Tenement house.

Kebbuck (S) Whole 'cake' of cheese.

Tulzie (S) A short skirmish.

Bastard Chevalier. A scurrilous reference to Prince Charles Edward Stuart, Bonnie Prince Charlie, and his claim to the throne of Britain.

Wheen (S) A motley collection.

Gillie. Attendant. (G) *Gille*, boy or servant.

Brown Betty. A nickname for a musket.

Kail runt (S) Cabbage stalk.

Fontenoy. A French victory under Marshal Saxe against the British, the Austrians and the Dutch during the War of the Austrian Succession (1745).

Sib (S) Bound by ties of blood or loyalty.

Sell. Saddle.

Groat. Small value coin.

Girnel (S) Storage chest for meal.

Firkin. Barrel.

Brog and Turk. Nicknames, Shoe and Boar.

Vaunting. Boasting.

"Aora Mo Chridhe tha mi seoladh". "Aray, my heart I am sailing".

II

Wae (S) Sorrowful.

Change-house. A place where travellers changed horses.

Rouse. Waking up.

Tom-an-uardar (G) Hillock of the timekeeper (not shown on maps) in Glen Aray by which the time could be told from the shadow cast on it.

"Crodh Chailein". "Colin's Cattle", a very lovely 17th-century lullaby.

Plack (S) A small coin.

Partan (G) Crab.

Clabbie-doo. Horse-mussel – much larger than the ordinary one. Literally "blackmouth", (G) *clab*, big mouth, *dubh*, black.

Giley and Hake. Types of fish.

Barking. The fishing nets were soaked with tanin (from bark) to prevent them rotting.

Horoyally. A good time, an evening of merriment.

Hector, Gilean-of-the-Axe and Diarmaid of the boar's snout. Clan heroes. Gilean was the eponymous founder of Clan MacLean.

Guddle. Catch fish with the hands, either under banks or in shallow pools.

Gauger (S) Exciseman.

St. Molach. Celtic saint St. Moluach. Some objects belonging to Highland saints were believed to have magical powers, including sprouting new life. The crozier of St. Moluach, long held at Inveraray, is now in the keeping of Alastair Livingstone of Bachuil, on the island of Lismore, the hereditary keeper of the relic.

Culloden Moor. The final defeat of the Jacobites at Culloden, near Inverness, in 1746, when the Hanoverian army defeated Prince Charles Edward Stuart's clansmen.

Garron. Highland pony. (G) *gearran*.

The Irishers. There were Irish soldiers in the Jacobite army at Culloden.

Keening. (G) *caoineach*, lamenting.

III

Bicker (S) Beaker i.e. strong drink.

The withie. A peeled branch, generally of willow, which was sometimes placed across an open door to signify that the person inside did not want to be disturbed.

Spirtle (S) Spoon or stick for stirring soup or porridge.

Ben. Back

Tansy. Flowering herb, looks like Ragwort.

Loth. Reluctant.

Kilachatrine. The churchyard of St Catherine. The modern St Catherines across Loch Fyne from Inveraray.

Routh (S) Abundant.

Caileag bheag (G) Little girl.

Pudding. Sausage-shaped or round-shaped food item made from blood and called by the Scots black pudding. (G) *marag dhubh*.

Dunedin (G) Edinburgh

"Slochd-a-Chubair gu bragh!" "The Cooper's Pool For Ever". The Cooper's Pool was a nickname for Inveraray.

A Fine Pair of Shoes

Awmrie (S) Cupboard, pantry.

Gangrel (S) Wandering person, often a beggar.

Snod (S) Trim, neat.

Unco. In this context, awesome.

Baldi. Diminutive of Archibald.

Crom (G) Bent, crooked.

Brog. Awl.

Kail (S) Cabbage.

Crouped (S) Crouched.

Lapstone. Last.

'Illeasbuig. Vocative form of *Gilleasbuig*, Gillespie. Used as equivalent of Archibald.

Tormaid (G) Norman.

Glen Falloch. A glen at the north end of Loch Lomond.

Spang (S) A short space or stride.

Bauchel (S) Worn out shoe.

Castle Dark

Wood Mamore. An estate on the Gare Loch belonging to the Argyll family.

Corbie-stone (S) The flat, step-like stones on the gables of some Scottish houses and called corbie (crow) stones because crows perch on them.

Birlinn ghorm. Gaelic for blue barge or galley.

Gentle or semple. Gentry or commoners.

Iorram (G) A boat song to set the rhythm when rowing.

Airt (S) Direction.

Mactallamh (G) Echo. Literally "Son of the Rock".

Crotal (G) Lichen which was used for dye.

Eachan (G) Usually *Eachann*, Hector.

My Lady's Canter. A hunting path near Inveraray Castle.

Trews. (G) *triubhas*, trousers, but close to the shape of the limb, like modern leggings.

Morag (G) Marion.

Chirming (S) Chirping or warbling.

Tirrivie (S) Tantrum.

Stour (S) Dust

The Black Bed of MacArtair. A carved oak bed of the MacArthur chiefs now in Inveraray Castle.

Bere (S) Barley.

Cartes (S) Playing cards.

Dover. Doze.

Lave (S) The rest.

Snell (S) Harshly, bitingly.

Yont (S) Beyond.

Jus Primæ Noctis

Jus Primæ Noctis was not included in the 1896 edition of *The Lost Pibroch and Other Sheiling Stories*. The publisher William Blackwood declined it on the grounds that it was somewhat risqué. It was, however, published in W.E Henley's periodical, the *New Review* in 1897. It was later included in the posthumous Inveraray Edition, *The Lost Pibroch, Jaunty Jock and Ayrshire Idylls* (Blackwood, Edinburgh 1935).

Ealasaid (G) Equivalent of Ailsa in this story, but more usually used for Elizabeth.

Hagbut. Old-fashioned hand gun.

Sculduddry (S) Indecent.

Creel (S) Deep basket.

Infield and outfield (S) In the early agricultural system before enclosures and crop rotation were introduced the infield consisted of the best land nearest the farm buildings which was kept continuously under crop and well manured; the outfield was the outlying and less fertile part of the farm.

Tack (S) Tenancy.

Lot. Piece of land allotted to a particular tenant.

Croft. Smallholding. (G) *Croit.*

Junk. Perhaps a shortened form of junker, meaning an aristocrat.

Cailzie-cock. Cock capercaillie or wood

grouse. (G) *capull coille.*

Lutzen. Battle (1632) in the Thirty Years War in which the Swedish King Gustavus Adolphus, champion of the Protestant cause, was slain. The narrator of this story was one of the Scottish mercenaries fighting in his army.

Buff. Military coat.

Posting (S) Tramping.

Boyne (S) Washing tub.

Limmer (S) Hussy

Kirtle. Petticoat or skirt.

Other One. The Devil.

Tacksman. Chief tenant and therefore a collector of rent from sub-tenants.

Arches. This reference to the screen arch in Inveraray which extends from the Great Inn across the Dalmally road is an anachronism. It was built in the 18th century, designed by Robert Mylne. This story, however, appears to be set in the late 16th century.

Stalacaire (G) Usually spelled *stalcaire,* stalker.

Rhuadh (G) Here the spelling should be *Ruadh.*

Bladair (G) Spokesman, often also flatterer.

Withie (S) Basket made from willow wands.

Doune pistol. Thomas Caddell set up business as a gunsmith in Doune, Perthshire, in 1646. Such was the quality of his pistols that they became famous all over Europe.

Thig stoidh (G) More usually spelled *thig a stigh.* Come in.

Arraghails. Argylls. Adapted from the phonetic rendering of (G) *Earraghaidheal,* Argyll. Literally, the coastland of the Gael.

Kerched (S) Wearing a kerch or kerchief on the head.

Mass. This reference suggests that the story has a pre-Reformation setting which is inconsistent with the information that the narrator of the story had taken part in the Battle of Lutzen in 1632.

Mutch (S) Cap worn by women.

Deiseilwise Left to right. Munro's own footnote should read "sunwise". From (G) *deiseil* which means southwards or lucky.

Kebur. Rafter. (G) *Cabar.*

Cess. Tax

Ifrinn (G) Hell

Craignish. Craignish Castle, north of Crinan, a seat of a sept of Clan Campbell.

Duineuasail (G) Gentleman. More correctly, *duin'-uasal.*

Jalouse (S) Suppose, suspect.

Acknowledgements

This edition of the *Lost Pibroch* collection has been based on the text of the Inverary edition (1935).

The Notes were compiled by Rennie McOwan and Rae McGregor assisted and advised by Alastair Campbell of Airds, Lesley Bratton, Rev Dr Roderick MacLeod and Liz Paterson.

Particular thanks are due to Lesley Bratton, grand-daughter of Neil Munro, for her generous advice and help with biographical and other details for both the Introduction and the Notes and for her enthusiastic encouragement of the whole project.